"Why don't you and us step outside?
We got business to discuss."

Slocum sat ever so still. In that same raspy voice
he said, "I ain't no rustler. I dream about the men
I killed. I don't want you in my dreams."

"Well, I don't suppose you got any choice..." That's
what Mountain Jack said just as all hell broke loose.
Mountain Jack had expected trouble, he was primed
for trouble, and he had one hand on his pistol butt.
But Slocum's table crashed into his knees so hard
Jack folded over it. Slocum was wounded but he
had strength to spare. That table came up like it
was steam-driven, and Mountain Jack just flipped
over it and, quick as that, John Slocum laid a pistol
next to his ear...

OTHER BOOKS BY JAKE LOGAN

JAKE LOGAN

GUNS OF
SOUTH PASS

BERKLEY BOOKS, NEW YORK

GUNS OF SOUTH PASS

A Berkley Book/published by arrangement with
the author

PRINTING HISTORY
Berkley edition/March 1984

ISBN: 0-425-06846-3

A BERKLEY BOOK ® TM 757,375
Berkley Books are published by The Berkley Publishing Group,
200 Madison Avenue, New York, N.Y. 10016.
The name "BERKLEY" and the stylized "B" with design are
trademarks belonging to Berkley Publishing Corporation.

PRINTED IN THE UNITED STATES OF AMERICA

1

The flies warned Jessica of a change in the weather. Two plump flies batting against the dugout's only glass window. The other windows were oiled butcher paper with thick wooden shutters in case of a storm. Sometimes Jessica and Lacey were so weary they didn't bother to open those shutters even when there was no storm danger and the dugout would stay dark, except for the light through the one twelve-by-twelve glass window like a cyclops above the dry sink. The flies were fairly sluggish and their buzzing was erratic but they batted against the glass trying to get into all the light they saw outside.

The back of the dugout was in the bank and the roof was continuous with the slope of the hill. It had been a prospect hole once. Their mother had bought the dugout from the man who turned the simple hole in the earth into a home.

Though the fire was long out and the chill remained in the back of the dugout where she and her brother slept, the front of the dugout faced south and the sun had warmed it enough to set the icicles to dripping and hatch the two flies.

Jessica watched them, unsmiling. "The blue-eyed Indian gal" was what they called her in town. She wore long johns,

1

socks, and over all that a heavy flannel nightshirt that had been her mother's. Lacey snored, gave a gasp and a cough, then his regular breathing resumed as she padded about gathering pine cones and dead grass and pine slivers to fire up the stove. Though the stove was too small for the dugout— just a sheepherder's stove with a couple of burners to heat up water or coffee or keep a stew pot bubbling—they never seemed to have enough wood for it. With both of them working, it was hard to find the daylight hours when they could get down the old two-handed bucksaw and fell, split, and transport the firewood back to the cabin. It would have been easier if they hadn't had to drag the wood through three feet of snow. But, of course, if it hadn't been for the snow, they wouldn't have needed the wood in the first place.

They'd been worried about firewood for five months now. They were never more than a few sticks ahead of the next storm. But this morning, when it was warming, Jessica felt a sense of relief wash through her. She felt the warmth of that sun in her bones and built a small fire to heat water for tea.

Jessica Tripp was just fourteen years old, her brother Lacey two years younger.

The flies crawled against the glare. The pattering noise outside was melt water dripping from the icicles onto the ice. It sounded almost like rain, the patter was so fast.

It was early morning, two miles east of South Pass in the territory that just last year had been created—Wyoming Territory. To the west was the enormous reservation ceded to the Sioux, Arapaho, and Crow. They were supposed to stay on their reservations and no doubt some of them would. In winter, for sure, they stayed there. The inhabitants of South Pass, all fifty-three of them, would stay in place, too. Once the snow came, only a madman or an imbecile would try to travel through the Wind River Mountains at 7800 feet above sea level, which was the elevation of South Pass itself. The town, named after the pass, was twenty miles north and a thousand feet higher. Nothing moved. Mink, marmot, marten, and jackrabbits danced on top of the crusty snow and the birds hopped around the chokecherry and service berry bushes hoping to find one shriveled, winter-hard berry for food.

But no humans moved, nor oxen, nor draft horses either. The beaver and the grizzly were denned up. The deer and elk and buffalo had trampled yards in the lower meadows where they pawed through the snow for sweetgrass or peeled the bark off the cottonwood or quaking asp. They couldn't travel through the snow any better than man could.

Today the snow in those yards was slushy and soft. The grass underneath was pale green—not the lush green of spring, but as though a thread of green was sewn inside each blade of translucent grass, coloring it.

The dugout was fifty miles from Point of Rocks on the Union Pacific railroad. Point of Rocks was 226 miles west of Omaha.

The sky was the brilliant dark blue of high altitudes. It glared against the billows of snow which surrounded the tiny home. Jessica used some of the tepid water to wash her cracked and roughened hands. The remainder was poured into their stoneware cup, the one without the handle. She preferred China tea, but only had jars and jars of dried camomile which she gathered last summer. The camomile cost nothing.

Her brother grumbled in his sleep and turned on his side and drew his knees up toward his chest. The warm mug cupped in her hands, Jessica stood over him and allowed herself a smile.

Her mother had had no more than thirteen summers when James Robbin Tripp had taken her for his bride—his third, but her only husband. That was back in the fur-trapping days. He'd first spied the Snake Indian maiden at a rendezvous at the Jackson Hole. Nobody knew it then, but that rendezvous was one of the last the Mountain Men

were to enjoy. The world had changed beyond their reck-
oning. That lack of foreknowledge didn't prevent them from
enjoying the rendezvous. They'd come to Jackson Hole to
drink, fight, and screw, and that was what they did.

Though James Robbin Tripp took religion in his later
years, in those days he was something of a ladies' man.
His first wife, a white woman, had died in childbirth in
Indiana. His second, a Pawnee, had died of lockjaw, James
Robbin Tripp thought, from spending too much time fooling
with the horses. That was, he believed, his fault, since it
was a man's duty to care for the horses. A woman should
clean the hides, salt the elk, and give comfort to her lord
and master. She should not fool with the horses no matter
how much she loved them. James Robbin Tripp had heard
of other men getting lockjaw from horses but he'd never
heard of a woman getting it before. She had died in agony.

So James Robbin Tripp came to the rendezvous looking
for a woman, never guessing that Gull Woman would be
his last.

She'd been a skinny thing, eyelids and cheeks reddened
with ocher, black hair pulled back in a knot. Her hair came
to her knees when loose. James Robbin Tripp came to love
Gull Woman's hair.

He bought her for three ponies, ten beaver pelts, and a
flintlock rifle. The rifle had been old when he first bought
it. Gull Woman's father had lost an arm to a Crow arrow
in some forgotten war and was, consequently, a poor hunter.
To the crippled warrior, three ponies, ten beaver, and a long
rifle was big wampum.

Gull Woman was flattered at such a good price. It proved
her husband was a good provider. James Robbin Tripp created a brief improvement in Gull Woman's place in Indian
society.

Gull Woman was afraid the first night together. She knew
what to expect. She'd heard her parents' lovemaking in their
modest lodge. But she had known this white eyes for only

three days and she'd heard that white eyes sometimes ate their wives, starting with their privates. Of course, Gull Woman had laughed at this story when it was told to her, but the white eyes were pretty strange—and who could tell?

Her passageway was too narrow. Though she obediently lay down on the fur floor of her new lodge with her kindly new husband; though she spread her knees as far apart as she could and squeezed her eyes shut so she wouldn't be frightened, her pelvis was locked tight. He pushed at her and it seemed to her that there was no opening there at all. He pushed and pushed until she slid back on the bear rug and opened her eyes and tried to place him herself. It didn't work.

He rubbed his cock with bear grease and knelt again and centered himself and pushed and Gull Woman lifted her hips to present a fair way, but still he hurt her and withdrew.

He said, "I knowed you was a virgin, but had hoped to alter that unfortunate condition."

Gull Woman smiled a scared smile because she didn't understand her husband's language yet. She never would come to use it very well and after James Robbin died and she became a whore, her poor English retreated still further. Near the end she conversed with her children entirely in the Indian tongue of her people.

Jessica spoke the white man's tongue well. Lacey, who'd been nine when his father died, spoke better Snake than English. He claimed it hurt his mouth trying to twist over all those sharp American words.

Jessica tugged the blanket higher on her brother's shoulders and he muttered in his sleep. *Let him rest,* she thought. *He'll be working again soon enough.*

Bundles of camomile and dried herbs hung over the dry sink. Their frying pan and one-quart tin pot dangled above the stove. Jessica hung pictures cut from *Vanity Fair* and *Godey's Lady's Book*. Pictures of ladies in bustles, a Florentine palace, a large circular engraving of Abraham Lincoln, the Great Emancipator. Jessica knew what all those words meant, though she had only just started to read.

She'd fastened the pictures directly to the dugout's square-cut log walls. Stuck them right to the logs with bits of gray oakum chinking. They fluttered every time the door opened.

Since James Robbin Tripp had been unable to enjoy his new wife at the rendezvous, he nearly sent her back to her parents and demanded his gifts—horses, beaver, and rifle. But, for his time, James Robbin was a kind man, so he beat her with a stick instead.

Gull Woman rode behind her new husband when they left the Jackson Hole. The mountains towered above her. In May they were still covered with snow.

James Robbin Tripp made no further attempt to sleep with his new wife. He didn't beat her again, either. He expected her to cook his elk steaks and buffalo hump and showed her how to brew coffee. He showed her how to make soda bread a dozen times before she got the hang of it, but he showed great patience. Except for business, he didn't talk much. One afternoon, three weeks down the Platte, camped at Sandy Springs among the bull grass and bunch grass, she took off her dress and unbraided her hair and lay down for him, and they took great pleasure in each other and in the world.

Though they were together as man and wife after that point, Gull Woman didn't present him with a child until three years later when Jessica was born. Two years after that, Lacey was born. Lacey was a colicky baby and he came down with pneumonia. Only the constant attentions of Gull Woman and James Robbin Tripp pulled him through. After the fur trade collapsed, James Tripp guided immigrant parties. He was a perfectly capable guide and knew the Oregon Trail as well as any man, but he was inclined to be surly and when the wagons collected in Independence or Omaha, most of the scouting jobs went to men with less knowledge and a little more charm, men like Bridger and Jim Colter.

Gull Woman accompanied him on his first trip. On his second trip, Gull Woman and baby Jessica traveled with him too. On their return trip, solo, her knowledge and quick tongue probably saved their hair when they happened across a bunch of Crow along the Upper Salmon River.

After the War, the west changed abruptly, radically, and permanently. The telegraph lunged across the country following the immigrant routes. James Robbin Tripp shot meat for the telegraph crews.

The wagons hurried west: horse-drawn, mule-drawn, ox-drawn. Once when the Mormons weren't able to supply enough animals for an immigrant train, they supplied the train with two-wheeled carts. Humans, men and women alike, were to draw these carts across the mountains and deserts ahead of them until they reached the gates of God's new kingdom on earth. Those fortunate enough to draw these carts reached God's new kingdom in heaven rather sooner than they had hoped.

So many travelers—thousands, tens of thousands, a hundred thousand over the Oregon Trail; more on the Bozeman Trail, forcing the war tribes back on themselves.

During the War, for the first time in history, the tribes had regained ground the white eyes had taken from them. They overran camps and whites burned their forts before they ran.

Captain Fetterman lost his entire command to the Sioux and the remaining soldiers cowered inside their fort and cried for help.

But after the War ended and the western flow recommenced, the Indians fell over themselves in retreat.

South Pass in 1869 was the very edge of that retreat. Just fifty miles north, at Camp Stanbaugh, sixty soldiers waited out the winter as locked in as the Indians were.

James Robbin Tripp had known the beautiful Rockies as only the Indians knew them. When the railroad started pushing west, Tripp took religion, prayed, and died, leaving

Gull Woman, Jessica, and Lacey Robin Tripp. On his deathbed James noted that he didn't have many belongings to leave and no family or friends whom they could abide with. He would trust to God for their care. Gull Woman sold his watch to bury him. She kept his genuine Hawken rifle. And she became a whore.

Gull Woman wasn't pretty. Her face was somewhat hatchet-shaped. Her hips were prominent and her breasts small. She never pretended affection and never took anything from the lovemaking for herself. Many men found her hauteur irresistible. Sometimes they gave her two bits, sometimes half a dollar. Since hard-rock miners were bringing down two dollars a day, two bits was not bad money. It was enough, anyway, to pay for their grub and to buy a secondhand, too-small sheepherder's stove for the dugout.

When South Pass was booming, sometimes Gull Woman would have half a dozen visitors during the day and in the early evening. She never saw anyone after the evening star came out and she never forgot two of her English words: "No fuck."

After James Robbin Tripp got religion, but before he died, he read Bible passages every night to his family. Usually he read from the Psalms by candlelight, forming the difficult words slowly on his tongue. Both his children listened avidly, Gull Woman much less so. But until the day two years later when she followed James Robbbin Tripp to the grave, every night when the evening star came out, she lit a candle and set the Bible on the crate that served as their kitchen table.

Once when Jessica reached out to touch the book, her mother became quite angry, striking her and calling her a devil child.

After her mother died, Jessica opened the black book, looking for the sounds of her father's voice, the beautiful things he said, but all she saw was squiggles marching across the pages in some indecipherable order.

Miss Sallie Arthur was teaching Jessica to read. Miss Sallie had once been her mother's competition in South Pass. Now she was Jessica's friend.

The tea warmed Jessica's stomach no less than the bright sun warmed her skin. Motes danced in the square of bright sunlight and Jessica could count half a dozen living flies.

She shook her brother's shoulder. "Wake up, lazy boy! The sun is shining and melting the snow, and we'll be fortunate to be at work on time."

Sleepily, Lacey rubbed his eyes and snorted. He was always sullen when he woke and even the sunlight didn't bring much life to his face. He threw the covers back and set his feet into his boots. He wrapped the blanket around him and clumped over to a chair beside the stove. He warmed his hands over the hot metal. He looked at his sister's hands. "Thanks for making me coffee," he said grumbling.

"We don't have coffee. And you don't like camomile tea."

"I like the sassafras tea."

"But we used up the last of the sassafras roots weeks ago."

He stood again, went to the window, and eyed the flies. When he made a snatch, his robe fell from his shoulders. "Ha! Three at once!"

"Yes," she observed. "You are a real man, as anyone can plainly see."

Her brother had learned none of the white man's modesty. In the summer, if he wanted to take a swim, he peeled off all his clothes, no matter where he was or who might see him. In town, when he felt the urge to relieve himself, he stepped outdoors, and didn't care who he scandalized. Now he sat down buck naked and grinned at her. "But you're my sister," he said.

"It is not proper for a brother and sister to see each other when they are no longer children," Jessica said primly in the Snake tongue.

Her brother grumbled, but he got dressed. He had neither the Indian modesty nor the white man's. He had the worst of both worlds.

After her mother died, Jessica took down the blanket that had separated the children's side of the dugout from their mother's. Though the blanket was perfectly usable, Jessica burned it. She burned it in memory of all the afternoons when they'd hidden outside, despite the weather, so they didn't have to listen to what the white men did to their mother on the other side of the blanket.

Jessica had sworn she would never be a whore. She would starve first.

She took a hunk of stale bread, cut it in two pieces, and spread it thickly with lard. Breakfast. Jessica salted her bread but her brother preferred his plain.

Their dugout faced due south and was just two gulches from the gulch which contained the town of South Pass. The South Pass of the Oregon Trail, that's what they named the town; though the actual pass was miles to the south, a low hollow in the Rockies where immigrants looked at the down side of the continent. "Is that all there is?" Immigrants asked each other incredulously. It wasn't. They still had the long haul through arid wastes ahead of them, and many more would die before they reached their destination. On South Pass, for a moment, they were delighted at the long, soft slope before them and the illusion that all their troubles were over.

There was a good spring at South Pass, Pacific Springs. Clear water and plenty of it for all the people and animals in the immigrant train. Travelers hoped they might flow west just as easily and inevitably as the water from that spring until they too would stand in the water of the Pacific.

No more than five miles to the east was the gold reef they'd named Miner's Delight. Still further east were the tents and shanties of Atlantic City: population five or ten, a much less promising discovery than South Pass and, God knows, the heart had gone out of the South Pass find soon enough. It had been a boom town for precisely one summer. Near autumn most everybody left after scoring the hillsides with empty gopher holes and destroying every gravel bank along the muddy creek.

The creek never was much. Not much water in it, slow-moving, sluggish. It could hardly power a sluice box, let alone all the sluice boxes of all the miners up and down the stream and water for horses and men, too, though many men didn't drink anything weaker than beer from year to year.

It had been scouts from the early Oregon trains who first discovered gold in the blue, broken quartz above South Pass. They brought samples of fine gold back east and said they'd been lucky to get back with their hair, let alone return for gold, no, sirree.

Jessica Tripp dressed carefully and wore a heavy wool scarf, though it was really too warm to wear it once she was moving.

Through the winter they'd kept a trail open between their dugout and the town. It didn't matter to them what kind of gold others found at South Pass. They'd never see any gold and precious little silver. She made seventy-five cents a day, her brother made four bits. They could eat leftovers and they could take the occasional stale loaf home.

The coming of the U.P. railroad emboldened prospectors to search the hills around South Pass with more courage than their predecessors. A high plateau at the tail end of the mountains, just scrub brush, clay underfoot, and sagebrush. Not much vegetation. A few pines on the east slopes and some cottonwood and mountain ash in the river bottoms. The sawmill in the town perished for want of good timber to feed it.

The trail from the kids' dugout to town was indirect. It

kept to the lee side of the ridges, very near the top, and only descended into the gullies to cross them. On the lee side where the wind shallowed and hardened the snow, a trail was easy to keep open. In the gullies, snow could get far over their heads unless they jumped from boulder to boulder.

The glare was terrible. Lacey and Jessica put on leather eyepieces with the tiny pinprick holes for snow goggles. The pinpricks let in enough light but didn't sear the sensitive retina. If either one of them went snowblind, how would the other get him or her to warmth? If they both went blind they would die in their tracks.

Bare slopes like white haystacks. Sometimes, at the very top, the snow curled like a breaking wave and here they trudged in the shadow of that snow wave under the cornice where it was shallowest.

When dry, the snow was stable and not awfully slippery. Now their feet skidded or slipped at every step and the sheer pleasure of the warmth was soon lost in wet leggings and boots filled with slush.

A chinook warmed them. That southerly wind that sometimes visits the mountains in late winter to bless them with warmth. A day or two, the wind would hold, often less. It came as a promise of spring, but many took it for the real article.

As the crow flies, the dugout was a mile from South Pass, but the trail was five miles. Six days a week they walked it, always together. Though the hours of their work were not identical—Lacey started and quit earlier than his sister—they always traveled together. Twice they'd been caught in blizzards. Once they'd made it to the dugout, where they were snowed in for forty-eight hours before they could even try to return to town, employment, food, warmth. During the other blizzard they had holed up with Sallie Arthur in town.

They walked ridges single file, casting long shadows

down the gullies. The sun glinted on icicles hanging from the slick rock. They walked carefully. A bad fall would be unthinkable. A thorough wetting might chill them to death.

Snow collapsed off the brush clumps, spattering and marking the snow beneath like a shotgun blast.

They saw a plume on the face of the distant mountains like a great gust of wind. It was the crash of the first spring avalanche, a great spume of snow that swept down ancient tracks, shattering what had rooted since the winter before. The two watched the plume and, a moment later, heard the rumble, like the growl of mountain devils.

Lacey wore a miner's short rubber coat over two layers of sweaters. He wore baggy pants stuffed into a miner's high rubber boots. Jessica wore a plaid mackinaw with a gaping rip in one sleeve, heavy fur-covered mittens, a pair of the miner's denims Levi Strauss made, and high moccasins. She wore her scarf slung carelessly over her shoulders. With her circular dark glasses, she looked like a blind man.

They knew every hazardous place in the trail. Their progress was steady, though sometimes quite slow where the footing was icy.

A pair of ravens circled high above the pines on the eastern slope. Snow tumbled off a cornice in a fine wet spray that dampened Jessica's mackinaw, and still they walked. The walk took two hours on good days when the weather was clear.

They might have moved in closer to town, but their mother was buried beside the dugout. The kids and Sallie Arthur had dug the grave and said the words over the poor pathetic body wrapped now in her last stained sheet. They'd put a tin can at the head of the grave and they kept wildflowers in the can. During the winter it filled to the lip with snow.

The can was the final marker for Gull Woman's grave. They had never thought to mark it with a cross, a symbol about which the children had mixed feelings. Because of her father's reading, Jessica would have preferred a cross, but her brother said no, and Lacey had known her mother's mind better than Jessica, particularly in those last months when Gull Woman became an Indian again.

They walked in silence, each lost in thought, until they surmounted the ridge that overlooked South Pass.

South Pass was digging out of the winter. Though the boardwalks in front of the abandoned buildings—LIGHT-BURN & CO. GEN'L MERCH., BILLY WILSON'S SALOON— were snow-covered yet, some enterprising souls had cleared most of the others and the street was bare all the way from Johnson's Livery to Paxton's Inn, the largest and most graceful of all the buildings in town. The street was frozen scraped dirt. It hadn't begun to melt. Laundry and blankets hung from second-story porches. Jessica recognized Sallie Arthur's vivid quilts hanging from the balcony of the Paxton Inn. She and her brother had slept under those quilts when they'd been stuck in town.

South Pass had a few boosters, but none of them claimed the town was beautiful. Some, William Paxton among them, admitted that it was ugly as warts, just a sprawling parcel of buildings beside a sluggish, shallow creek.

But boosters claimed the quartz was pretty. Pretty enough to make up for the ugliness, the harsh climate, the isolation, the real danger from the Indians. The quartz was bluish and rotten. The gold was wire gold winding through the mouldering quartz like hot veins in a dying body.

The merchants had been in a great hurry to build South Pass. They bought logs right off the sawmill, tacked them to the green studs, and slapped a coat of bright paint over the whole thing. They generally did business while the interior was quite incomplete: parceling groceries, nails, or flour while the carpenters hammered and carried more lumber past the customers. Since the wood was green, it had shrunk and checked and curled as it dried. It wasn't a big problem on the occupied buildings, but the abandoned stores had spaces where boards had simply curled right up and fallen off. When somebody made off with the wood for firewood, the gap was made permanent.

The snowbanks on both sides of South Pass's main street were higher than Jessica's head and snowmelt sent puddles sliding across the frozen dirt. It would be a real mess when it came time for them to go home.

They split up at Paxton's. Lacey was the swamper; his job was to clean out the spittoons and sweep the old sawdust into buckets. Mixed with a little kerosene, used sawdust made dandy fire starter. He lifted the duckboards and mopped behind the bar. He took chairs down off the tables and stacked chips and laid out fresh decks at the hexagonal poker table.

At noon, he set out the free lunch. In the fall, when South Pass was fully populated, his work kept him busy, and sometimes he'd bring out three or four platters of the free lunch—dill pickle, rye bread, ham, elk haunch—but since most everybody had left, one platter often lasted two days now.

Six hundred miners, teamsters, millers, carpenters, engineers, reverends, gunslingers, and drummers. They'd left, most of them, when the gold ledges at South Pass didn't pan out as rich as first seemed. Besides, just fifty miles south they were putting a telegraph through and wages on that crew were steadier than most could make from a prospector's pan.

The Clarissa ledge still produced gold. It provided steady work for three muckers, a driller/powder man, and a boy. Major Wright who opened the Clarissa ledge, continued mining ore, though he couldn't extract any gold from it until spring.

It had been the miners' most serious complaint about South Pass: the two or three good gold ledges didn't have enough water for a sluice. At some gold strikes enterprising

souls would construct a wooden flume from some far-off
water source and lease water to the miners for their sluices.
A couple of men had talked of doing that here, but nothing
had come of it.

Lacey swept the chilly saloon. He'd built a fire in the
potbelly, but the heat hadn't reached very far yet.

The curled horns of a bighorn sheep adorned the back
bar. Beneath it, floor to ceiling, a nine-foot-tall grizzly pelt
was stretched. Rows of glasses, bottles of identical rye
whiskey in unlabeled green bottles, bottles of bourbon in
clear bottles. Paxton's had sold the last of its beer in January
and though they had barrels working, the weather had been
too cold for the beer to brew.

Upstairs, Jessica Tripp was doing her lessons. Sallie Arthur was a whore but she'd been a schoolteacher once and
she listened to Jessica read as she fluffed her bed, shook
her curtains, and dusted.

Sallie was a good-looking woman, full-breasted, with
blond hair. Men found her easy to be around, comfortable.
She'd tried to get respectable a couple of times but had no
particular luck at it. She wasn't much of a cook, couldn't
deal poker or faro, and wouldn't clean rich folks' homes.
She'd thought about respectability quite a bit five years ago
when she was still in her twenties, but now she rarely thought
about her choices.

"That word is 'Calvary,' Jessica. 'Cavalry' is soldiers.
'Calvary' is the mountain where Jesus died."

Sallie Arthur taught the girl from two books: *Favorite
Shakespeare Plays,* edited by Bowlder, and the King James
Bible.

Jessica closed her book but left her finger in to mark the
page. "We have forty-five dollars," she announced. "I
counted it last night."

Sallie had watched as the Tripps' grubstake grew a week
at a time, inexorably, predictably, toward its goal. The fare
from Rock Creek to Omaha was forty-nine dollars on the
brand new Union Pacific Railroad. Forty-nine dollars wasn't

much. Even a couple of half-breeds could save that much. Three trains a day arrived at head of track: immigrant, passenger, and freight. They'd leave in April when the trains began running again.

"Forty-five dollars!" Sallie pretended surprise. "That's a bit more'n I thought you had." Sallie noticed the thinness of the girl and the brilliance of her blue eyes. Most of that saving had come from not eating, Sallie thought. Poor kids could eat scraps that came back into the kitchen. And generally they could eat a little of the leftover free lunch. William Paxton never gave much thought to the youngest and smallest of his employees and, if he had, no doubt he would have said, "I pay a fair wage. If they're hungry, I pay them enough to eat. Day's work, day's pay."

William Paxton didn't know what it was to dream of leaving these high barren mountains, to go back East where a woman had some opportunity—any opportunity. Perhaps Jessica could become one of the new woman secretaries, or a bookkeeper, or work in a dry-goods store. That was Jessica's dream, and her bright hungry eyes wanted that dream more than food.

"Just four more dollars," Jessica said. "And then we'll start saving Lacey's fare."

"I thought Lacey didn't want to go back East. I love this sun." Sallie held up a frilly yellow blouse in the light streaming through the window. She had her window open. It felt like sixty degrees outside. Men called back and forth to each other on the street. Men who'd been huddled around a fire for months were outside today, and no surprise if a couple of them pelted each other with snowballs. There were whoops and shouts.

Sallie interrupted Jessica's look of disdain. "Just foolishness!"

"All men are fools," Jessica said in a flat voice. "Drunken fools. Lacey will come East with me because I take care of him."

"Another couple years, he'll be carin' for himself," Sallie

noted. "And you won't be taking care of anyone unless you learn to read better than you do. Now you open up that Shakespeare again. I want you to read me through Polonius' speech again."

As the girl stumbled through the unfamiliar words, her brother moved through the bar saloon setting the room. He never minded working alone. He didn't mind the sweeping or the cuspidors either. That was just work. But when a white man spilled his drink or puked, and Lacey was called to wipe up the mess, he took it personally. And the miners, who were not over fond of Indians, inevitably made remarks meant to be overheard and Lacey's ears burned. He would have happily cleaned twice as long if he hadn't had to be on call for the barroom.

At eleven-thirty Paxton's man, Vinegar Varese, made his appearance, striding from the lobby into the saloon bar. He checked his hunter against the regulator clock and nodded his satisfaction. Vinegar dressed like a swell. His shoes were neat, his vest fawn-gray. His bowler was gray too and tilted on the back of his head. His face was incredible.

Vinegar Varese was built like a passenger pigeon. Big in the chest, spindle-shanked, he carried himself so far forward he seemed over-balanced. During the War, as a loader for a Dalgren gun, he caught the full back blast that blew the breech open. It shriveled and pocked his cheeks, exploded his eyelashes, melted his nose and ears. He should have died from his burns, but instead he just got mean. He grew into the full strength of his manhood, big bones, big frame, with hands the size of ham butts. His mouth had been crudely pasted over his teeth and had no real expression. Just the words that came through the same scarred hole he also breathed through. He was a frightening man to look at, and most men spoke to his shoulders or his shoes rather than his eyes.

Sallie Arthur, who had seen the naked male form in many

shapes and sizes, and wasn't too particular, slept with him just once. Twenty dollars Vinegar paid for a night, and by sunup, at seven-fifteen A.M. in January, Vinegar had had his money's worth. Sallie Arthur didn't even come out of her room for two days. Jessica Tripp left soup and tea for her on the landing just outside her locked door. When she did reappear, her walk was stiff and sore, her eyes glazed over with real pain.

The following weekend, while Sallie was taking her ease with a couple of admirers in Paxton's saloon bar, Vinegar Varese walked over to the cozy table and wordlessly dropped a double eagle. The coin bounced and rang and everybody looked at it and at Sallie Arthur's eyes, Vinegar's countenance being so generally horrible that nobody looked at him.

Sallie Arthur's face went dead white under her professional paint. The irises of her eyes were enormous, dark blue. She went into her reticule for a pistol. It was a gambler's pistol, a Philadelphia derringer. It held just one little .38 caliber ball. She aimed it at Vinegar's blistered forehead and said, "I'd die first." Most of the customers in the saloon took Sallie's part. Though she never extended any man credit, she'd never given less than her best. She was known as "game." Nobody cared for Vinegar Varese. Hell, most men couldn't stand looking at him. But nobody voiced their sympathies too loudly because Vinegar was the bartender and bouncer at Paxton's and had been known to cripple a couple men and everybody had heard the rumors of corpses along his back trail.

He was very big. He carried a length of ash club, three feet long and as big around as a silver dollar. He never carried a Colt, was never known to use a knife. He just beat men with his hands and his ash stave.

When the population shrank, things got stable in South Pass. Men knew each other and everybody, except one woman and one man, feared Vinegar. The woman was Sallie

Arthur, who was willing to die or kill him, which elevated the stakes from a casual romp in the hay to a feud Vinegar took seriously. The man was William Paxton, who was once identified in the *Cincinatti Inquirer* as a boy genius. Paxton paid Varese for loyalty, a relationship both men understood.

Vinegar growled something at the swamper, went behind the bar, and poured himself a pick-me-up. He polished a few glasses and ran his finger over the back bar looking for dust. He wound his hunter.

Because the day was so beautiful and so fine, naturally many miners decided to get drunk. The men who'd been bombarding each other with snowballs trooped inside, laughing and joking. One miner claimed he saw miners from the Clarissa hauling ore to their sluice, hoping for enough water to thaw.

"Yeah," another remarked. "Maybe the Major's getting tired of paying men who aren't earning a flake of gold."

"Wouldn't it be a joke if all the Clarissa ore was pure country rock, no gold in it? They'd never know until they sluice."

"I'll drink to that."

Idle miners get fretful and restless. Men who seek the favor of the quartzite and granite aren't over patient at the best of times and after a winter of being pent-up, unable to work their properties or prospect, hearing the same lies over and over, listening for the thousandth time about the flume that failed or the new six-stamp mill Miner's Delight was expecting come spring (when that order had gone out in November—*November*, for Chrissake), they got testy and impatient.

There was something frantic in their exuberance, the nervousness of men who have one leg unchained but not yet the other. They drank more recklessly than usual and the crowd was bigger than usual for an afternoon. Lacey Tripp returned three times to the kitchen for more free lunch. His sister was scrubbing pots in the scullery. When she was done, she'd hurry upstairs and fix up Mr. Paxton's rooms once he descended, which he did each day precisely at noon. Paxton wasn't yet twenty-five years old but he moved like a man with brittle but serious authority. He was soft-spoken, eager, and always looked on the bright side of things. He often advised others to the same course.

He was rubbing his little hands together as he came into his own saloon and a stranger could be forgiven for mistaking him for one of those clockwork devices made in Europe, those mechanical men sawing at miniature violins or performing to the music-box strains of Strauss's latest waltz. He smiled and shook the hands of men he'd seen last night or the afternoon before with the enthusiasm of a man making first acquaintance.

William Paxton's genius was real estate. He left the details of gold mining to others. He was perfectly content to own the main street of South Pass on either side except where Johnson's Livery had got in before him. As recently as January, he'd made an offer to Johnson's Livery which had been, to Paxton's disappointment, refused. He still shook Johnson's hand whenever he saw him.

William Paxton was waiting for the spring when all the miners would return to his town and find more gold and make him very, very rich. He asked of Vinegar Varese only that he do what he was told to do.

Paxton shook Vinegar Varese's limp grasp. "It looks like spring is coming early."

One sly old grubstaker lifted his eyes from his glass long enough to remark, "I seen killing blizzards in this country in June."

Paxton stopped rubbing his hands and smiled. "Why, if it were to snow today, the snow would simply melt, melted by the sun as it fell. Gentlemen, I'll stand a round and a toast: to spring!"

That caused a minor flurry of business as everybody got a free one and everybody raised their glass to Paxton, too, because who wouldn't have wished, as he did, that spring was here. But they all knew better.

Upstairs, Jessica Tripp was making Paxton's neat bedroom neater. She remade his chaste bed, closed the closet door on his wardrobe of four identical suits in differing weights but identical shades of gray. By his orders, she didn't straighten the desk by the window with its scraps of paper, piles of deeds loosely tied together, stationery from the South Wyoming Land Co., the South Pass Hotel, South Pass Mercantile, and the stationery that simply said *Wm. Paxton, esq.*

She took his laundry—one shirt, one celluloid detachable collar, one string tie, one set of men's drawers. She also brought his water pitcher. William Paxton had been often heard to exclaim that the water in his saloon was the best water this side of Pacific Springs and, as a measure of his loyalty to his own ideas, he drank nothing else. He wondered aloud if this water, which did taste a little sulphurous, might not have some curative qualities. Just a hundred miles north and west, the fabled yellowstone hot springs poured forth their curative effusions. Might not South Pass's water possess some of that water's magical properties?

Sallie Arthur swept into the saloon somewhat grandly. She asked for a glass of sherry and took her customary seat at the table nearest the window.

Plenty of fast chatter. Men drank, worked themselves up with their own talk and the beautiful weather.

Paxton counted heads and signaled Vinegar to keep the free lunch coming.

A couple of miners sat at the poker table but quit after three hands. They ordered another round. Johnson, of the livery, sat down with Sallie and bought her a drink. Though Johnson smelled a little horsy, he was a regular customer, a gentle man with a long, awkward face and long, awkward hands. She said, "Thanks for the drink, pal. Ain't it just fine today?"

Johnson agreed.

Men can't stand too much happiness. Even Vinegar Varese was trying to quell the sheer pleasure of the day with more than his customary amount of booze. He'd kept right up with his customers and his scar flexed and twisted and a vein pulsed above his right eye, like blood under red mica.

Vinegar Varese was restless. Cooped up all winter in his small room and only slightly roomier barroom. Sell the bottles and the shots, collect the money. He tossed off another shot of rotgut rye whiskey and, for the first time, he really saw Jessica Tripp. Something in the graceful way she walked caught his eye and he stood behind his bar utterly transfixed by the vision of the young girl with the water pitcher.

He had never seen anything more beautiful. The girl walked softly, quickly to the pump and lifted one slender arm to work the handle. She didn't take the first gush, but filled her pitcher with the tailings.

It was raw admiration moving him when he came up to her, put his arms around her waist, and whispered, "I'll have you. *You.* I give fifty dollars, gold."

Her face was startled. She spun from his arms and the pitcher struck the back bar and shattered. A heavy, curious silence fell and all eyes were on the big man and the little girl he had cornered at the wet sink.

She looked at him. Not at his face, at his eyes, and he, who was used to fear and revulsion in the gaze of others, saw nothing in her gaze but sheer puzzlement, as if what he'd suggested made no more sense than the mating of a donkey and a swan. What he suggested was simply impossible.

"I go now. You have caused me to break Mr. Paxton's pitcher. You may find him another and place it on the bedside table. He prefers water from this pump, as you know."

Somebody snickered. Vinegar Varese clenched his fists.

He tried to make a joke of it. As she left the room he said, "I'd give you a gold double eagle just to shuck your clothes without you havin' to *do* anything." His voice died with the last few syllables.

2

For three lovely days William Paxton had it all his way. The sun melted the snowbanks into themselves. The ice withdrew from the roofs, the roadsides, the edges of boulders in the field. The Clarissa had enough water running to operate the sluice six hours one day. Usually a sluice is only cleaned once a week but the boys working the Clarissa hadn't seen paydirt in so long they cleaned every hour, running their heavy magnets over the black sand that gathered in the riffles, coating the magnets with a heavy black fur and leaving nothing in the riffles but flecks, nuggets of gold, and sapphires the size of matchheads. The sapphires weren't gem quality so they threw them out with the magnitite, the black stuff on their magnets.

Each bit of gold was brushed into the Major's poke and that evening the whole crew came into Paxton's for a ceremonial weighing. One day's sluicing had produced nearly two pounds of pure native gold. The miners were a little disappointed. Three pounds at fourteen dollars an ounce was the goal most of them had had in mind, but two pounds wasn't that bad and if the weather stayed warm, they'd sluice again tomorrow.

The Major, who'd invested a chunk in the stamp mill scheduled for delivery in the spring, was most relieved of all and drank the heaviest.

In fact, William Paxton sold quite a bit of liquor in those warm, bright days, days that seemed like a holiday. Nobody but Paxton expected the good weather to last and some of the more provident souls took advantage of the warmth to get out and cut firewood.

The trail between the Tripps' dugout and South Pass was slithery with slush and deep water in the gulches. Water had started to roll under the deep snow and every morning and evening the kids had to ford a four-foot snowbank with feet and ankles in icy rushing water.

They removed their boots and crossed barefoot. Wet boots would mean a full day of misery. They each owned only one set of footgear.

They struggled into town every morning and, in the late afternoon, struggled back to the dugout. In the evening, Lacey whittled or played solitaire with a deck missing only two spades and a diamond. Jessica studied. The harder things got, the harder she studied.

She did think about Vinegar's offer. She didn't think how it would be to sleep with him, but how fifty dollars, with the money she'd already saved, would buy them both a ticket East to the land of opportunity. Fiercely she studied, practicing her words with a piece of charcoal on a flat pine board, tracing each letter with scrupulous care.

The road thawed. The trail between their little dugout and Atlantic City and Miner's Delight thawed, too, and one day a couple of bearded miners from those diggings passed by the door on their way into town. The miners had a bad case of cabin fever, were surly and quick to take offense. They meant, they said, to spend the rest of the winter in a more civilized setting.

The next morning William Paxton saddled a tough little mountain horse and he and Vinegar Varese rode south all the way to the South Pass. They returned in the early afternoon, soaking wet, on exhausted, shuddering horses.

Snowbanks and torrents. Every gulch was full of runoff and in all the spots the sun hadn't touched, the snow was as deep as ever. Paxton was very discouraged and developed a nasty head cold.

Sallie Arthur was taking two and three men into her bed every night. In the coldest weather all desire dies. When it warms, then the blood starts flowing. Sallie had her "regulars," her "occasionals," but now she was getting the "rarelys."

Winter had enclosed Sallie, wrapped her in its icy chill. In February she'd just made enough to pay for rent and food for herself and the scraps she slipped the half-breed kids. In the first days of the chinook, she paid the next month's room rent in advance.

Through his stuffed-up nose, Paxton said, "The road's almost passable between here and South Pass. It might be better on the other side. A determined man could get through to the railroad."

"Yeah," Vinegar replied, "and how would he get back here if the weather changed? He'd be stranded in Point of Rocks until iceout."

Paxton shook his head. "It's an early spring," he said nasally.

Vinegar went to the window. He looked at the sky, which was becoming overcast. "I hope you ain't throwed your long johns away," he said.

In the kitchen, Lacey was helping his sister scrub the last big pots. The cook never scrubbed a pot after the night meal and by the time Jessica got to them the contents had the consistency of cement.

"You go out and get our money," Jessica told her brother. Jessica didn't like to be in the same room as Vinegar Varese.

The big man couldn't take his eyes off her. Vinegar Varese thought he was smiling at the girl, but since most of his mouth was fixed in a scar, his smile wrinkled one of his red cheeks and stretched the end of his upper lip. It was like no smile Jessica had ever seen.

William Paxton handed Lacey a silver half-dollar. The half-dollar had a woman on the face and a big eagle on the reverse. Lacey thought the white man's money was odd and he examined every coin he was given. Rather reluctantly, Paxton fished out a quarter for Jessica. All winter long he'd been paying out without taking hardly anything in. Oh, the saloon paid its own way, and three of the twelve rooms in the hotel were occupied, but he had salaries to meet and Vinegar Varese depended on him. Like many employers before and after, William Paxton thought of the work others did for him as no more than what they owed. He thought of their wages as pure generosity on his part, like he was doing them a kindness.

"Are you finished in the kitchen?" he asked the boy.

"Yes."

"The upstairs hall was dusty yesterday."

"I'll see to it before we go."

Vinegar Varese was watching the clouds. "Here comes winter," he muttered, and poured himself a shot of rye.

Perhaps it was only imagination, but Paxton felt something—a chill in the air, a draft. He shivered and pressed the quarter into Lacey's outstretched palm without benefit of the homily he was prone to utter on such occasions.

At the window, Vinegar Varese was shaking his head gloomily. A couple of miners muttered curses. Another, at the bar, downed his drink and departed hurriedly.

The two children hurried up the back stairs to say their farewells to Sallie Arthur. This was usually a perfunctory routine, more a checkout than anything else, but today Sallie had something else in mind.

For the past three weeks she'd been altering a boy's shirt

to fit Jessica. It was all wool, cut generously. Sallie had
shortened the sleeves, repositioned the buttons, and let the
shirt out in the bust to make room for Jessica's swelling
breasts.

Though his sister naked was nothing new to Lacey, he
had to wait out in the quiet darkened hall while Jessica tried
it on.

Jessica was so surprised a tear started. She squeezed it
back. She'd vowed when her mother died that nothing was
ever going to make her cry again. Certainly not kindness.

Sallie Arthur pretended not to notice. She stood with her
back to the window. Swollen clouds whipped by and the
water dripping off the little icicle that hung from the outer
frame slowed, grew sluggish like it was oil, and stopped.

"You'll be nice and warm in this," Sallie said. Stripped
to the waist, Jessica looked more womanly, though her ribs
were prominent and the shelf of her hip was a knob. Her
breasts were a little larger than Sallie had expected and she
was glad she'd left the shirt roomy in the bust.

"I hope you're not allergic to wool," she said.

With eager fingers, the girl buttoned the heavy shirt.
"Oh, no," she said. "Sallie, this is so warm! It's wonderful."

"Paxton said he had a bunch of boys' clothes over at
Lightburn's. None of the men in town are little enough to
wear it, but it fits you fine. They've got some woolen boys'
long pants, too. Only trouble is, they're bright red."

Jessica preened herself before Sallie's full-length mirror.
During business hours the mirror was tilted at the foot of
Sallie's bed, but otherwise she kept it against the wall like
a proper mirror.

The girl's work-roughened fingers clutched the heavy
warm shirt together at the neck. "Oh, it's so nice. Sallie,
thank you. You're so good to us."

Sallie wrinkled her nose. "Now remember what I told
you. I want you to start memorizing those Shakespeare
sonnets. I don't care if you don't get what they mean. You

will by and by. Just memorize a sentence at a time." Just then a blast of cold air rattled her window in its pane. The sound sobered them both.

Jessica let go of her new shirt and scanned the sky. "Yes. Those are snow clouds," she remarked.

"Do you have food at home?" Sallie asked.

Jessica shrugged. "Enough." What they had was yesterday's loaf of dry stale bread, some tins of tomatoes, and the camomile tea.

Sallie took the girl affectionately by the shoulders. "Johnson. You know him?"

"Sure."

Sallie gave her a burlap bag. It must have weighed close to ten pounds. "Bear haunch," she explained. "Johnson doesn't hardly ever pay in cash. He always leaves me these little presents. It's sweet meat, but I can't eat bear. It gives me hives."

"Sallie, you are kind to us. More kind than our mother."

Sallie turned away and made a vague gesture. "Go on now. Get out of here. Get home before the weather sours. Now don't forget, you got plenty to eat for both of you. You don't absolutely have to come into South Pass. I don't want to find you froze to death in the snow."

Solemn little Jessica replied, "Sure. Be seein' you." And she was gone.

Sallie watched them out of sight, Jessica hurrying, her brother with the sack of bear meat slung over his shoulder. Already they were leaning into the wind. Sallie lit her kerosene lamp and pulled the curtains. She sought the warmth of the glow.

The zero wind gusted and blew. It sought the entrances in the kids' clothes and sucked the heat away from their bodies. They hurried just to stay warm.

The slush had frozen into brittle ridges and milky-colored ice. The ice stood in the snow like lakes in a snowy wood. The snow ridges were crusted, sharp, and dangerous where the wind had frozen them.

It was half an hour from the South Pass to the top of the first ridge. They never looked back at the friendly lights and warm rooms so close behind them. They had too much distance to cover.

With the snowmelt stopped, the first gully was better than it had been. They didn't need to remove their boots and socks to wade through the snowy water. The facing slope was so slick it was almost impossible. They went up the glaze on hands and knees, using their own frozen footprints for hand- and foot-holds.

Near the top they huddled for a second just below the wind licking at the bare places. The clouds were much lower now. They could see only a hundred yards. The clouds were fog and wetness and would soon be snow. It was dim enough that they didn't have to wear their makeshift snow goggles.

"We aren't getting home squatting here," Lacey said and scuttled half upright into the wind, clamping his hat down on his head and slinging the bag over one shoulder.

The wind nearly knocked Jessica down. She took an involuntary step sideways, slipped, and sat abruptly. She felt a chill of fear. Suppose she'd sprained an ankle or twisted her knee in its socket? Lacey hadn't seen her fall and he'd already started down into the second gully. Feeling like a fool, she scuttled to her feet and hurried after him. Her knee hurt, but she could walk. She *would* walk!

Lacey plodded on ahead, placing each foot in turn on the frozen slope. Both fell, Lacey twice. Each time they caught something or punched a hole in the snow crust, or they would have slid and skidded all the way to the bottom. Lacey scraped his knuckles when he fell and the blood was there right at the knuckle. Lacey wondered why he bled so much more when he was half frozen.

For a couple of days Lacey had been eyeing a dead pine which had been exposed by the chinook. With snow coming, he figured he'd take a few minutes to gather fuel. The pine, lightning-struck, had toppled sideways onto its own branches. The trunk was hollow, black against the snow, but the broken branches stuck through the crust like dragon's teeth. Lacey rocked a branch back and forth until he could free it from its icy trap. He moved to another. Some of the branches came easily. Some were so locked in ice they couldn't be jiggled.

"How can we carry all this?" his sister asked.

"Just hold them at the big end and drag them behind you. We don't have any wood at home."

Jessica was tired and cold and the blackness in the sky spelled storm to her. The thought of a warm dugout encouraged her to pick up three heavy pine branches, each of them considerably longer than she was tall. She dragged along in Lacey's footsteps, glad for the slick, thick crust on top of the snow. She tucked the butt ends of the branches in the crook of her arm and pulled with her whole body.

The two half-breed children hauled their makeshift travois.

The first snow came so wet and so fast it blinded them. It melted off their faces but stayed on Lacey's muffler and hat and Jessica's turned-up collar. One of the branches jerked out of Jessica's grip and she had to set the other two down and align them again before she could proceed. In the gully bottom they followed the main trail, frozen but, except for recent dusting, still clear of snow, and the poles clattered easily along behind them. They hurried now, so near to dark, so close to home. The trail was wide enough here for the two of them to walk side by side.

"Bear meat," Lacey Tripp said loudly.

"Good fire," his sister giggled.

The two of them broke into a trot. It was slippery for running and the poles bounced along behind. Both of them were laughing.

No light in the dugout, and the stink of a long-dead fire.

It was as cold indoors as out, and Jessica didn't mind when Lacey left the door open on its leather hinges as he broke and carried the wood in.

The wood was dry and shattered easily where he whacked it with their splitting axe. It was but a moment's work to get a fire roaring. Jessica scooped the teapot full of snow and set that on top of the burner plate. The kettle hissed and popped for a second before it settled down to melting.

When the wood was in and the fire roaring, then they shut the thick door and fastened the drawstring. The silence was sudden and large. Lacey took off his wool cap and beat the snow against the stove. "We'd better hang our coats to dry. It's gonna be a hell of a storm."

"Don't curse," she said mechanically. Somewhere along the line she'd got the notion that if she could be educated, her brother could be educated, too—a noble proposition but, given the depth and intensity of Lacey Tripp's resistance to correction, an unlikely one.

With oakum stuffed in all the cracks, the dugout was pretty tight. After Lacey scratched a couple of candles into life it was bright, too. Jessica drew her curtain across the glass window, closing the dugout from the world. Jessica's curtain was a piece of feed sack on a string. Her candles were bowls filled with tallow with cotton strings for wicks. One of the candles rested on a shelf above Lacey's bed. The other, with a tin-can lid reflector, lighted the kitchen table.

Lacey hadn't had a chance to admire his sister's new shirt earlier. Now he fingered the cuffs and collar. "That Sallie," he said. "She . . . oh, hell!"

His sister made a face at the language but agreed with the sentiment.

Brother and sister were alone in the high-country storm. Outside the snow flurried and drifted. Inside, Jessica sliced bear steaks. She licked her fingers. They were fifty miles from the railroad, three miles from another human being.

They might as well have been on the moon.

They ate their steaks and heated canned tomatoes, and the bread didn't seem as stale as it usually did. Paxton's cook hated to bake and wouldn't throw old bread away until it was dead stale.

Afterwards, over tin cups filled with scalding tea—Lacey didn't even complain about the camomile tonight—they spoke about what they'd seen that day.

Lacey spoke often about Vinegar Varese. He'd become fascinated by the man after the offer Varese made to his sister. At twelve years of age, he didn't feel obliged to tackle a grown man over an insult, but he watched Vinegar Varese like a hawk. He spoke of his gait, the way his big hands were held at his sides. "He never lets them just hang there. He always has them cocked, like he expects to fight. I'd think they'd get tired that way, but it don't seem so."

In a small voice, Jessica said, "Please don't talk about him any more."

His hand rested on hers. "I won't let him hurt you," he said. Her quick smile was accepting, not quite believing.

Jessica washed their two tin plates and dried them. They owned just one good bowl, two plates, and three cups, including the cup with no handle, but Jessica always kept them washed and dried. It was her way of imposing order in the wilderness.

Lacey sat on the edge of his bed blowing softly into his harmonica. The harmonica had all the notes except one at the top and two side by side in the middle, but Lacey knew songs for which those notes weren't very important. Lacey could play the "Rose of Alabama." He could play "Skip to my Lou" and "Yankee Doodle Dandy." He knew the yearning chords of "Shenandoah," and he played that refrain now as Jessica settled down with her Shakespeare.

The way Shakespeare spoke was like the way the Bible spoke and if Jessica couldn't puzzle a word until she could figure its meaning, she closed her eyes and imagined her daddy saying words from the Bible. Sometimes that would make the understanding come.

She said the sonnet aloud, under her breath, making a kind of purring sound. And that was how it was there in that lone dugout cabin on the upper reaches of the trail between South Pass and Atlantic City. A girl murmuring, a young boy playing the harmonica, the sputter of the tallow candles, the pop and crack of the fire. The sliding sound.

Jessica looked up right away, but Lacey had his eyes closed, playing his harmonica. He'd found it in saloon saw- dust last summer after a rowdy Saturday night.

The sliding sound wasn't particularly loud, but it was big against a few feet of their outer wall. It was like tree branches rubbing a wall or roof in a thunderstorm. Soft, though, like it wasn't the branches rubbing, just their soft leaves.

The words of the sonnet still paraded through her mind like words painted on the backdrop of her eyes. She raised one hand for silence. Lacey heard her sharp "Hush!"

"What's wrong?" he asked.

"You hear that?"

"Hear what?" Lacey cocked his head.

"There. That sound. Like there's something out there. Like something rubbing."

Lacey grinned, "Maybe it's a bear. A big old bear!" He put both his feet up on his bed and played the opening bars of "Stonewall Jackson's Way." His instrument didn't have notes for the rest of the song, but he was learning to play around them.

"It does sound like a bear." It was a soft, brushing noise. Jessica got up and went to the wall, as if hoping to hear better. That wall was in the lee of the storm. Maybe some animal had gone back there to escape the snow's fury. Sometimes even tiny animals could make a terrific noise. All last summer they'd had a packrat under the floor. Some-

times, when Jessica was nervous, the sound of his scamp-
ering had kept her from sleep, sounding loud as a kettledrum
in the house.

No. This might have been an animal, but it wasn't a
small one.

Lacey put down his harmonica. "Maybe it's some brush
been picked up by the wind."

"Listen. Was that a clinking sound?"

"I dunno. I dunno what it is."

Rather coolly she said. "I believe Daddy's Hawken's is
charged."

That got the boy's attention. Quickly he lifted the old
rifle off the wooden pegs that held it. "She's ready," he
whispered.

The rubbing sound came again, this time much deeper,
like whatever it was out there was pressing hard against the
outside logs. Jessica put her hand on a log and felt a slight
vibration, or so she thought. "Perhaps it is the People," she
said in the Snake tongue, meaning her mother's people.
"They will not know who is inside—red or white."

In the same language the boy replied, "It might be Crow
or Sioux or Shoshone. It might be Sheepeaters, driven out
of the mountains by the avalanches. It might be—"

"Hush!" She put her finger to her lips. Both of them
could hear it now: a jingling. Definitely a jingling.

A pine bough popped in the snow. The girl jumped. The
boy twitched and his neck got red.

"Well," he said, annoyed, "I ain't gonna be spooked by
noises all night. If it is a bear, then we ought to shoot it,
and if it's a Crow or a Sioux, we ought to shoot him, too.
It's too wild a night for lengthy discussion."

As if to punctuate his speech, the metal chimney rattled
where it passed through the roof. The wind was playing
with it again. Though Jessica would have sworn she had
sealed every crack in the dugout with oakum, her kitchen
curtain ruffled in a draft.

"They may be waiting for us right outside the door," Jessica suggested.

The boy had no patience with her fear. He never did have patience with her fears. They'd been too close to death too often. Living as they did, they'd been close to death a hundred times from animals, men, or simply back luck and bad weather. "Get the kitchen knife. If there's any stabbin' to be done, that'll be your work," he said shortly.

She did as she was told. "Maybe it's just an old buffalo come up here out of the storm," she suggested as she wrapped her scarf around her exposed neck. She'd sewn their thumbless mittens, and they looked it. Each mitten was two plate-size pieces of bear hide, fur side in. She'd made some attempt to follow the outlines of the human hand, but she was far too unskilled to chance a thumb.

"I hope it's a buffalo," the boy said, pushing his rag-wrapped feet into his boots. "If it's a buffalo, we'll have enough meat for spring. Just poke the hams and chops in a big old snowbank and cut off the meat whenever we want it. Wouldn't that be grand?"

"If it's the People," she said in a whisper, "you do the talking."

He grunted his assent.

Butcher knife in hand, she stood by the door with her hand on the latchstring. By clamping the lock against his side, Lacey was able to cock the overslung hammer with a tiny click-click as he drew past the half-cock stop. He put the rifle to his shoulder, aimed for the center of the door, licked his lips, and nodded.

If some hostile Indian had been standing in the doorway Lacey's rifle would have been useless, because a blast of snow-laden air smacked him and he couldn't see or hear a thing.

The door banged against the opposite wall. Jessica's knife was at her side, forgotten.

In December they had had four bad storms. In January

one of the storms had blown for forty hours without ceasing. But this blast chilled them to the bone, standing protected as they were and only a few feet from a good fire. The door opened on a wild forbidding world.

Already, as they watched, snow crept across the door stop, seeking some peaceful, cold place to bank.

Angrily the boy stomped forward, rifle poking from his hip like a guide pole, one hand covering the hammer. One hand on the doorframe, he pressed his face into the howling wind and shouted a greeting in the Snake tongue.

He heard the howling of the wind, the blistering of his ears where nasty frozen flakes stung them.

"Hello!" he cried in English. "Anybody out there?"

The cabin light projected on the white, swirling snow like a magic lantern.

The rubbing noise was around the side of the house. Having come this far, there'd be no harm in seeing it up close. They'd sleep better if they did. He motioned to his sister and she followed, leaving the latchstring dangling on the outside of the door.

The wind came at their backs, steady as an ocean wave. They leaned back to keep their balance.

With the door closed, their eyes got used to what outdoor light there was, which wasn't much. Fifty feet away from the dugout on a whirling night like this you'd never find it again. The curtained light of the kitchen window glowed yellow on the boy's face as he edged forward. His sister followed almost exactly in his footsteps. She didn't know what the noise was, but she was glad it wasn't Crow. White men hated half-breeds; the Crows despised them. Last fall, just a mile out of Miner's Delight, a couple of Crow had caught a prospector and killed him. They cut out his finger tendons to tie their arrowheads and they used his back sinews for bowstrings.

Her brother's back was a blot in front of her. Already the blowing snow had found entrance at her neck and just above her waist.

Out here the rubbing sound seemed pure foolishness, some fantasy dreamed up beside the fire. She was cold. The wind was already taking the life out of her.

And her brother was gone.

Desperately she groped for the cabin wall, found the corner, and slipped around it after him.

He stood amazed.

In the lee side of the dugout, the snow fell slowly and gently. There was no wind to speak of, no roaring. Some pale moonlight made it through the storm.

It was a big horse, perhaps eighteen hands. It bore a rider, though the rider was as motionless as a statue.

Plumes of frosty air came from the horse's nostrils. The horse had its haunches against the logs of the cabin and from time to time it would start to slip downwards before it caught itself again. Ice hung from its belly hair and there was ice in its lanky black mane, and its ears were frosted. When the horse blinked, ice flecks broke on its eyelids. The ice around its wound was red and black. The wound was high in the rib cage and the dark blood had pumped out and hung in frozen rivulets from the animal's hair. The horse looked at them.

The rider was hunched forward in the saddle, his hat over his eyes, dead quiet. He'd tied his reins to his wrists and his fingers were twined in the horse's mane. Ice gleamed over the lump his hands made.

The horse snorted. Something flew from its nose and the horse groaned and opened its eyes very very wide, in astonishment. The blood gushed from its still nostrils in two streams. Buckets of blood poured through the horse's nostrils and open mouth and still the astonished eyes glared at them. The hot blood steamed and the horse's head was fogged like a mountaintop. Very delicately, it knelt, hindquarters still in the air. Again it groaned, a grunt, a sigh, and still the blood came, with less force but steadier. The horse's eyes got white, the color draining right out of them. It leaned against the log wall and crumpled. Its offside rear leg kicked, once, twice, then folded under its body, still trembling.

The animal lay propped against the logs, its rider's hands still wrapped in the mane.

Jessica moved first, brushing past her astonished brother. She had to think what to do.

He slumped forward in his saddle, his crotch against the roping horn. The horse gurgled and a tremor shook its entire dead body, but the rider rode it out, as indifferent to the motion as he'd been to the stillness. He hardly swayed.

Gently, Jessica reached out. His jaw was wrapped in a heavy muffler and only his cheeks were exposed. They were cold, cold as dead meat.

"Is he a dead un?" Lacey asked.

"I don't know." She'd jumped at her brother's voice. She'd forgotten anyone was here besides her and the ice rider.

Ice rimmed his hat and the back of his shoulders. Ice bristled the wool of his muffler and his pants legs, pressed against the barrel of the horse, were encrusted with ice armor. The wind started one of his spur wheels jingling and spinning. It was a faint little jingle.

She slipped his wide-brimmed plainsman's hat forward off his face. Where it wasn't ice-white, his hair was black. He sat upright, still motionless, eyes shut tight, locked against the storm.

She pulled her hand from her clumsy mitten and held it before his mouth. Was it her imagination? Did the faintest warm breath tickle the back of her hand? "He's breathin'," she observed.

"How we gonna get him into the house?" Lacey asked.

"Well, we ain't gonna do it jawing about it," she replied, though her heart sank. The ice rider was a big man, over six feet, and he looked like a real bundle to handle. Still, they couldn't just leave him here to freeze to death. She jerked at the reins. Frozen. With her butcher knife she sawed at the frozen leather. The reins were as much ice as leather and the butcher knife skidded several times against the horse's neck. It didn't bother the horse.

"Get some water," she said. "I can't get his hands loose with this knife."

Lacey hurried back in the teeth of the storm. It was funny how the storm didn't seem so fierce when you had something else on your mind.

The heat in the dugout weakened Lacey and he wanted to sit down, but he uncocked the rifle, returned it to its pegs, and snatched the kettle of hot water off the stove. Out in the cold the kettle steamed a modest fog cloud. Jessica cut through the reins and they dangled loosely from the ice rider's wrists.

"You're gonna scorch him," Lacey protested as she lifted the steaming kettle over the rider's locked hands.

"We'd best hurry," she said.

The first drops hit the icy surface of the back of the man's hands and spread and hissed. The next driblets didn't hiss and the hairs of the horse's mane gleamed glossily where the water thawed them. She scooped a handful of snow onto the rider's hands and poured the water through that. Maybe she could increase the temperature a little that way.

Big knuckles—knobby like they'd been broken. The webbing of the hands calloused by the reins, the thumbs big, the nails cut square across. She poured snowy hot water onto them until suddenly, convulsively, they jerked open.

She jumped back, but the rider hadn't moved, only his hands had jerked, and already they were filming over with ice again.

"Come on," she said impatiently. "Take him under the arm. Maybe we can drag him."

When they tugged, the ice rider came readily enough, crumpling over so he lay flat along his dead horse's neck.

The kettle had melted a hole for itself in the snow. "We're gonna have to get his feet out of the stirrups."

A man's booted foot is rather narrow. A stirrup is generally much broader, even the steel stirrups this rider favored. Why was it so difficult to push his foot out? It was almost like his leg had intelligence of its own, resistance, as though it kept trying to return to the stirrup. They poured the last of the hot water on his left boot and Lacey kicked at the toe while Jessica hoisted behind the knee to remove the strain. When the stirrup came free it dangled loose and the leg returned to the barrel of the horse as if, deprived of its stirrup, it meant to continue the ride bareback.

"His other leg. It's mashed there, betwixt the horse and the wall."

"You take him under the armpits. Go ahead. It's all right to stand on the horse. Just pull," Jessica urged.

He pulled. She pulled. But the leg vanished below the upper thigh into the crevice formed by the horse's side and the rough frozen logs. They couldn't even see the boot. When they turned loose, he coiled into his previous position, hands clenched like they were holding a mane, boot right where it had been.

"We can't thaw him," Jessica wailed. "We ain't got no more hot water."

"Here. Where's your kitchen knife?"

She pulled it out of the log where she'd stuck it.

He stabbed down with the knife, stabbed right against the horse's belly. The wound released steam from the horse's guts and a not-unpleasant smell of warm grass and hay. But the belly wasn't his target. Lacey was sawing with the knife through the heavy leather girth strap. The released warmth from the horse's interior softened the leather where he cut and he wiggled the thick-bladed knife through. "We'll take him stirrup and all," Lacey gasped. When the strap parted, neither saddle nor stirrup was bound to the horse, though the pressure of the horse against the wall still held everything in place. Lacey stuck the knife in another log. Whether the ice rider lived or died, they'd still need their only kitchen knife. "Come on up here," Lacey said. "Just kind of sit down. Put your feet to the wall and scrunch down so you can push the horse with your butt. We'll roll him away from the horse."

They strained. Jessica set her feet against the log and pushed, trying to roll the horse far enough to free the rider's leg. She pushed with her back and her knees. She put her all into it.

Lacey gasped, "If you can hold for a second, I believe I can pull him up now."

Through gritted teeth she said, "I'll try. Hurry!"

Lacey stood right behind the saddle, lifting the much heavier man under the armpits. His leg came out to the knee, to the ankle, then the boot, stirrup and girth strap pulling right along. Lacey tumbled off his perch, dragging the man with him. The back of the rider's skull conked him in the mouth and Lacey tasted blood from his cut lip. His sister was still sitting on the horse, not pushing, breathing in great heaves. Lacey tried to talk, couldn't, and made a weak wave.

They locked their arms around the rider's arms, hoisted him up by the armpits and walked away.

They'd pulled plenty of firewood through the woods. Last winter, when they had had a wooden sleigh, they'd pulled that, too. The man was heavier than anything. His legs dragged. They gasped as they pulled.

"It's the saddle, Lacey. His foot's still dragging the sad-dle."

Without the forty-pound saddle dragging behind them in the snow, their burden was manageable. Just.

They pulled four or five feet at a time, then sank down to get a breath. They faced back the way they'd come because of the wind. So near to being cheated of its prey, the storm had doubled its fury, and Jessica didn't dare look into the heart of the storm. Though they knew their own front door by long habit, Jessica fumbled along the smooth door for precious moments, groping for the latchstring.

It was a cinch to drag him inside, but both of them had to push to shut the door against the raging wind.

Jessica looked at what they'd rescued and her heart sank. The blown snow melted off her hat.

The ice rider lay on his side, still half curled up against the storm. His muffler had come loose in their struggle and his face was pale white with tinges of blue. ───

From his black hair he might have been Indian or white or half-breed like they were. It didn't seem to make very much difference now.

"Maybe he's dead," Lacey panted. For a moment, it seemed so futile that Jessica almost hoped he was dead. They both knelt beside the man. Outside they'd had no idea what he was—only that he was a man and not a woman. Now they could see that the ice rider was, or had been, a tall, lanky man with long legs and powerful arms. Pale as he was, he could have been any age between thirty and fifty. His hair was full and cut roughly. His eyebrows were as black as his hair. They both saw the pulse jump in his throat at the same time.

"He's still in the land of the living," Jessica said cheerfully, brushing all the cobwebs from her thoughts. "We'd better see about getting him warm."

"I'll put more hot water on the stove. Maybe we can heat up enough water for a bath."

"Use the big pot and the little one. Use the kettle, too."

"Aw, do I hafta?"

"Just go get it before you get so warm you fall asleep."

Lacey was back into the storm for no more than ten seconds but he was gasping before he put a kettle full of snow on the little sheepherder's stove. Snow in the big pot and the little pot. Snow in the sheet-metal bath that also steamed on the stove. It would hold five gallons of water, or a terrific heap of snow.

They found the wound when they had the rider's slicker

off. The sight of it made Lacey sick. The wound wasn't terribly ugly, just a neat, blood-rimmed hole in the man's shirtfront, but it was a surprise Lacey hadn't been ready for.

"Stop that foolishness, Lacey," his sister snapped. "Be a man!"

Lacey wiped his mouth and leaned against the door. "Jessica, he's gonna die on us. Can't you see that? He ain't gonna live, no more'n his horse did."

"This is where the bullet went in," she said, "but I don't see where it came out. Help me. I don't want to cut up his shirt."

But in the end that was what they did, cutting the dark blue flannel shirt to get it off his arms. His undershirt was so soaked with blood they had no hesitation about ruining it. With some of the water she had heated, Jessica wiped at his chest. The entrance wound was an angry-looking puncture that had closed up like a silent mouth. Jessica hated to look, but she rolled the man forward to see if she could find an exit wound.

"Isn't this it here?" Lacey inquired. Gingerly he touched a lump in the man's chest just under the skin like a knotted muscle, except no one had a knotted muscle on the front of his chest. "Maybe the bullet traveled along the rib cage," Lacey suggested. "Harvey Waters shot an elk like that last spring. When somebody else killed the elk this summer, it still carried the slug. Looked like that bulk elk was tryin' to grow tits." He jiggled the lump. The skin was hot to his touch, as if the bullet was still glowing.

"Put more snow on the fire," she said. "His hands are blue. We'll need water."

"We'll use up most of our wood," he warned.

"We've got a table, ain't we? And a wooden chair."

So Lacey loaded the hip bath and the pots with snow. Adding more snow to the water, adding snow to slush. The stove spattered as moisture hit the glowing plates.

Blue flannel thread and underwear thread was caught in the wound, and she picked carefully at it. With her brother's folding knife she cut bits of flesh away.

The ice rider was breathing regularly, but shallow and fast.

They cut his pants and underpants off him. Neither of them had steady enough hands to slip a knife between boot leather and his ankle, so they left the boots on. They hoisted him under the armpits and eased him into the warmth of the hip bath.

"Pour some of this warm water on his back," Jessica advised. "Trickle it. We're warming him, not washing him."

The man's black hair steamed when they poured water on it. One of his boot tops was just visible under water. The water reddened his flesh.

"What's this?" Lacey asked. He was pointing to wide stripes across the man's back. "Looks like this pilgrim's been whipped. I seen marks like that once. Jeb Wilingham, remember him? Surly bastard, walked funny. Said the whip had crippled him. He didn't have nearly so many marks as this man." He touched a wide mark gently.

While her brother sloshed warm water on the man, Jessica cut up some of their bear ham, just a little piece chopped fine with the butcher knife and fried it in its own grease, and poured a couple mouthfuls of tomatoes into the frying pan. No salt. No pepper. They didn't have any.

Patiently, she tipped the broth onto his tongue. Painfully, the tongue withdrew and both of them saw the man's adam's apple bob, just like a real living person.

Black hair on his chest and what looked like another ugly scar across his belly.

"This hombre's been hard used," Lacey said.

She got most of a cup of broth into the ice rider without him choking once, holding his mouth open with her thumbs.

Lacey removed his straw pallet from his iron bedstead. They laid the ice rider on the iron bedstead, snuggled up so close to the stove Jessica could hardly put her hand between. They gave him more blankets and quilts than they kept for themselves. They were bone weary and they'd done all they could. Live or die, it was up to the rider now, and there was no point wasting their little remaining tallow when a storm raged outside.

Lacey and Jessica lay down in her bed and hugged each other to sleep like babies.

3

Dawn wasn't much. Dim, cold mottled light ruffling the kitchen curtain. The floor was so cold it creaked and groaned when Lacey padded over to the stove. He gave an unhappy look at what remained of their pine wood. They'd heated plenty of water.

He shook down the ashes and set a couple of slender sticks on the fire before checking on their guest.

Still alive, breathing shallow. When Lacey touched his forehead it was quite hot.

Lacey hooked his fingertips in his armpits for warmth and hopped up and down until the new firewood caught. He laid his clothing over the warm stove, hoping to steal some of the chill, and scorched his shirt sleeve a mite, as he often did.

A broth of bear meat. Not so much bear meat left either, and some camomile tea.

He stepped outside to take a leak. When he opened the rude door, snow fell inside from the bank that had formed against the door. His sister uttered a complaint and he shut the door behind him. No use losing what heat they had.

Shafts of sunlight walked through the woods, interrupted

by swirling columns of fresh snow. It was quite cold, but
the wind wasn't so bad.

When he came back inside his sister was up and dressed.
Jessica had developed modesty along with her pubic hair.
Lacey had a few strands down there himself and he watched
them closely, waiting for reinforcements.

She had the remaining bear meat sliced into cubes. It
was to be another meat and tomato broth. No stale bread
left.

"I believe we're stuck here today," Lacey said. "Must
be near thirty inches of fresh snow. More still fallin'."

"We could use the snowshoes."

Lacey owned two pairs of much-repaired, narrow Indian
snowshoes—split ash laced with green deerhide. The shoes
were starting to spring apart at the tips and he was reluctant
to put much extra strain on them, but the extra strain wasn't
the reason for his refusal.

"Snow's too damn light," he said. "We'd sink right
through it until we hit old crust. It'd be four or five hours'
wading to get to town."

"Well, I think one of us ought to go. We can't take care
of him by ourselves."

The boy grumbled. What she said was true, but so what?
South Pass had no sawbones. The apothecary had left in
the fall taking all his nostrums with him.

She stirred the pot. "He's feverish," she said. "Awful
hot. What if he dies on us?"

"What if he does? He's just a stranger come in from the
storm. He ain't no kin to us."

"He is one of God's creatures, same as you and I," his
sister replied sweetly.

"Not me," the boy said. "I ain't." He considered himself
an Indian and held a funny mixture of Indian and Christian
beliefs. After his death he thought he'd wander in the shadow
land. And it would be a baby called "Babee Jay-su" who
would ultimately guide him out of that dreadful place. The

boy made a face at his broth. When you don't have a bite to eat, bear steak and broth seem pretty appealing. When your belly is full, broth looks uninteresting and bland. "I think I'll go outside and get his saddlebags. Maybe he's got something we can add to the pot."

He set them in the far corner where the melt wouldn't spread.

Despite herself, Jessica was just as interested in the stranger's gear as her brother.

Wrapped in a soft chamois cloth was a Colt, ebony-handled, browned octagonal barrel, very slightly oiled. It had been kept with the care normally given a very fine watch, and the gun seemed to have a life of its own. "He didn't have no rifle," Lacey said. "That's a Navy Colt, if I'm any judge." He hefted it, aimed it at the door, and his thumb touched the hammer.

"Put that down," his sister said. "It makes me nervous."

"Sure." The boy tossed the pistol on Jessica's bed.

Wrapped in a separate chamois cloth was a powder flask with one of those patented measures in the tip so it would throw the same charge of powder every time. A carton of conical bullets, caliber .36, and some linen patches. The percussion caps were # 9's and separately wrapped in a flannel bag. They found a folding cleaning rod, some brushes, a brass vial of gun oil, a tiny screwdriver, and a tiny file. "Well, if he does die," the boy observed, "we're richer. I'll bet I could get twenty dollars for that gun."

Two pairs of heavy shirts, one light green, the other dusty yellow. Both were worn but wouldn't need patching for quite a while. Four pairs of socks, each pair loosely knotted together.

"What's that?" Jessica asked.

Tin flask uncorked, Lacey took a sniff. "Whiskey. Pure whiskcy."

Pawing through the saddlebags he was like a kid opening presents under a Christmas tree. Long johns: two pair, one new. Rawhide laces, extra harness, some neat's-foot oil.

"Where's his food?" Jessica asked. "Man rides out in this country with no food is in a hurry to meet his maker."

"Maybe he had a pack horse and lost it. It looks like somebody didn't take awful kindly to him. That bullet in his chest ain't too old."

She said demurely, "I sniffed at the wound. It doesn't smell putrid, but it is awfully hot—his skin, just where the ball is—and I fear he has an infection."

"Maybe we could cauterize the wound," the boy said with a touch of eagerness. "Pour gunpowder into the wound and touch it off. That'd clean him up."

"Lacey!" she cried in horror.

"Well, it would. What's this?" Lacey had found a gold watch and chain wrapped in the toe of one of his socks. When he held it up, it spun and sparkled. "Real gold, all right." Lacey put it up to his ear, shook it, wound it, shook it again. "It's busted," he said. "I could have used a good watch. Say, there's something writ on the back. Maybe you can make it out."

CAPTAIN JOHN SLOCUM C.S.A.
Presented to him by his sharpshooters.

"So we know who he is, anyway," Lacey said after his sister had read the legend aloud. "Captain John Slocum C.S.A. That means he fought on the losin' side, right?"

Jessica was vague on the subject of the recent war. She'd seen none of it and none of her family had fought and she could perhaps be forgiven for closing her ears to the reminiscences and anecdotes of the terrible struggle which so recently had occupied the nation's energies. "I don't know," she said, prying a fingernail under the back of the case. "Look, he's got a tintype in here. There's a man and woman and two little boys. Maybe one of the boys is him."

She set the opened watch beside some of the Captain's

toilet gear, his comb and bar of yellow soap.

Lacey had a little trouble with the parcel that lay so neatly in the bottom of the saddle bag: oilskin, tied and cross-tied. Lacey lifted it with both hands and it was so very heavy that he guessed right away and lifted his eyebrows in wonder. "Well, I'll be." Urgently he picked at the knots and first one, then the other gave way to him. He unwrapped the oilcloth reverently and saw what the weight had readied him to expect. Four rows of gold pieces set on end. In the dimness of the cabin they gave little of their luster away, just glinted sullenly. The gold pieces were octagonal, not round, somewhat larger than a double eagle.

FIFTY DOLLARS
FINE GOLD
Jos. Adam's, Culler Calif.

"California gold. There must be thousands of dollars here. Jessica . . ."

"Wrap it up and replace it, Lacey," she said primly. "Our money is in the jar under the sink. We have almost fifty dollars."

Lacey was reluctant, but he wrapped the gold just as tight as he'd found it. "We don't get in today, ol' Paxton's gonna holler."

"Put the gold back in the saddlebag," his sister said. "Mr. Paxton will just have to fill his own water pitcher today." She raised her arms like an orator. "Healthiest water in the west, by God," she said gruffly, "a genuine fountain of youth." She giggled and, in a minute, the tension the gold had brought into the dugout vanished like the gold itself.

Captain John lay in the narrow bed, piled high with quilts and slept. Once, Jessica rolled back his eyelid, but she saw nothing but the very edge of the pupil. He sweated quarts and drank the warm broth Jessica spooned into him. It was

bear broth at first but it became horse broth after Lacey took
the hatchet outside. The horse hide was frozen and hard but
the meat underneath hadn't had a chance to freeze yet. Lacey
chopped the backbone above the hips and below the front
shoulders and whacked through the ribs. The red pillar he
lifted out of the horse was thirty pounds of good meat, a
fine loin. Lacey cut out both tenderloins and tossed the
scraps into the broth water. "We can eat good tonight,"
Lacey said, seeking some approval for the meat and all the
work he'd done to put it in their larder.

Jessica looked up. "Unless somebody drags some more
firewood," she said, "we won't be eating a thing. Burnin'
the table and chair is fine, but we're stuck here and they
won't last so long."

"Oh, all right."

It wasn't work the boy looked forward to, but his sister
had the right of it. Somebody had to feed the unconscious
Captain. Somebody else had to get the wood.

He didn't bother with snowshoes. No sense ruining them
with this work. Saw dangling from his shoulder, he plowed
through the snow to the nearest grove of pines, five hundred
yards away. One hour pressing against the unyielding stuff,
pausing for breath, creating a trench pathway, one leg after
the other plowing the snow. His pants soaked through where
his body warmth melted the snow. Soon the outside of the
pants froze again. From the pines the dugout looked like a
haystack covered with snow, a haystack with a chimney
trickling smoke. With a crosscut it was always awkward
sawing firewood alone. Though Lacey was strong for his
age, he'd been spending all his reserves, and he was only
twelve.

Back in the dugout his sister nursed Captain Slocum's
fever. She washed a grown man, hot as a racing horse;
washed his muscles and his skin.

The entry wound hadn't quite closed. It seeped clear pus.
The area directly above the bullet lump was hottest, but

Jessica could feel heat radiating from the wound too. She dabbed sweat from under his chin.

"Sure wish you'd come out of it," she said. "I'd surely like someone to tell me what to do."

Lacey retraced his path to the cabin with two pretty good saplings. He drank a full cup of camomile tea and played with the Colt Navy until Jessica said, "That ain't yours, either. You want to be playin' with something, go play with the crosscut saw." A sullen Lacey marched back into the snow for another weary load of wood. That was how the afternoon went, both of them working non-stop until the late shadows chased each other across the snow and the light cast a bluish shadow over the hillocks and pillows of snow.

Lacey was blind with weariness as he stumbled home one last time with three six-inch saplings and the saw tied across his own shoulders. He'd jerk at the saplings and they'd break loose and he'd plunge forward two, maybe three steps until he slipped or, usually, just ran out of breath and stood, his breath steaming like an overburdened dray horse. The dugout seemed very far away with the light pouring out of the hollows and hurrying to the hilltops for its last stand.

The sky was clear, with no more snow in it. The evening star had ventured out with several friends. Unless Lacey missed his guess, tonight was going to be bitter cold. It was always colder when the stars couldn't wait for the light to vacate.

The rectangular glow shone in the window. Lacey hoped they had enough tallow to take them through the night. Thanks to him, they had plenty of wood, and the thought warmed him for several more lunges against the hardening snow.

Captain Slocum still didn't wake. He ate easily enough, but he made no other human sign except for the tightening of his lips, just like a baby when he'd had enough.

Lacey fried up horse tenderloin for himself and Jessica. He burned it because he was an inexperienced cook and tired, but neither of them cared.

This night Lacey had the bed to himself while Jessica sat up with the Captain, washing him and feeding him every time she could. She dozed in the chair, waking if her charge tossed or the fire got weak. Once her patient frightened Jessica. It was the middle of the night and the tallow was almost gone. The Captain shouted a shout like no kind of call Jessica had ever heard before. It made her bolt upright in her chair, shivering. The Captain had his head thrown back and his body was board stiff from the back of his head to his heels. He was arching himself off the cot like it was red-hot. His eyes were wide open and just as white as they could be, no pupils in sight. His jaws were wide open and his teeth were grinding terribly, slow as a miller's stone wheel.

Lacey sat bolt upright. The Captain arched like a steel spring had expanded within him, like his soul was wrestling and his body was the battleground. Then he slumped as completely as he'd arched. He just melted back onto the bed.

"Babee Jay-su," Lacey said. "He dead?"

She touched his brow. "I don't think he's quite so awful hot as he was."

"If he's dead, we get all his money," Lacey said. "Maybe that's the death chill upon him."

She leaned her head to the Captain's chest. "No. His heart is strong."

"Um." Lacey scratched, yawned, and went back to sleep.

Next morning they waited until nearly midday before Lacey set off to South Pass for help. The sun was pretty strong and at this altitude, the sun didn't need quite so much time to do its work. By noon the fresh-fallen snow had melted and settled enough for the snowshoes.

Captain John hadn't said any more today than he'd said

yesterday. He was still sleeping when Lacey said goodbye.

Once again he wore the leather pinprick sunshield. And, though the snowshoes held his weight quite well, he traveled slowly. The slopes were twisted against his shoes and he feared the shoes just might come apart on him. He'd re-wrapped them this morning as best he could, using the Captain's leather laces. Jessica had opened her mouth to protest—she was so damnably honest—but Lacey cut her short by reminding her that the laces were being used for the stranger's own benefit. "I'm sure," he added sarcastically, "he won't mind. Hey, Captain, you don't mind, do you?" Lacey cupped his ear. The tin plate his sister threw banged on the door behind them.

He walked slow and cautious and in no hurry. When you could walk on top of the snow like this, walking was gentle. He walked above all the irregularities, the unevenness. He walked a frozen ocean all alone, with just the sound of his breathing and the thud of his snowshoes to break the silence.

He wore the snowshoes right up to the front door of Paxton's Inn. Paxton had shoveled the boardwalk in front of his establishment. The street was broken by the rude tracks of men and a few horses.

Paxton's kerosene glow looked pretty good to Lacey. He leaned his long snowshoes beside the door and hurried into the warm lobby.

Vinegar Varese was in the lobby. "Where the fuck you been?" he asked. "Don't think anybody's been doin' your work for you. You got a mess in there, and you better get to it." Vinegar Varese was chewing a toothpick which he rotated in his mouth.

William Paxton was behind the bar of his own saloon with a towel across his arm, just like he was used to it. The room was full of strangers. They gave Lacey the shivers and stopped his tongue. He knew every living soul in South Pass. He knew all about them. But Lacey didn't know these men.

They looked at him like he was fresh meat, like they expected him to do something interesting: to break into a buck and wing?

The tall gray-haired white man sported an old-fashioned formal coat, a ruffled shirtfront, quite elegant, discreet gold shirt studs. His hair was brushed straight back off his high forehead.

And the other tall man leaning against the saloon bar with his leg cocked on the rail—that must be his son, Lacey mused.

A squat man in buckskins was dressed like a mountain man except that he wore riding boots instead of moccasins and a white Stetson in place of the fur hat. This third man wore two Colts, butt forward, in military holsters.

"Don't gape, boy," Paxton snapped. "Go on about your work."

"Boy!" It was the languid man, the son, speaking.

"Yes, sir?"

"I'm looking for a man."

"Sir?"

"Black-haired man on a big Appaloosa. Five hundred dollars to the man who finds him."

It might have turned out differently if Little Will Japhe had had kinder eyes. But Bad Eyes held the half-breed boy up for inspection. Lacey Tripp had one single clear thought: he wouldn't want to be an insect under that indifferent, sneering gaze, much less a man. And the information bubbling in his throat was choked down. "F-f-f-five hundred?" he asked.

"Man called John Slocum. Haven't seen him, I s'pose?"

Lacey didn't trust himself to speak. He shook his head.

"Damn lazy half-breed hasn't been in town since the snowfall," Paxton observed. Paxton's blond mustache trembled with displeasure.

"But that's the point, don't you see," Japhe explained. "Had Mr. Slocum arrived in this town, we should have ferreted him out by now. Presumably this boy has been somewhere we haven't been able to search. Atlantic City, perhaps. Isn't there a camp at Miner's Delight? Miner's Delight, my Gawd!" He permitted himself a gust of laughter.

The older man's eyes were weary and flecked with red. His spine was ramrod-stiff.

Paxton said, "They've got a dugout just outside town. Him and his sister."

"A big man on a big horse. You've seen no sign?" The stocky man in buckskins spoke, "My name's Mountain Jack. Yours?"

"You want my Indian name or my white name?" Lacey said, hard as stone.

"Salty little bastard, ain't he?" Mountain Jack observed with composure. Wordlessly, Lacey went for his broom. When he went into the kitchen, he missed his sister. But Jessica had wood and meat. She'd be all right.

Like all swampers, Lacey was effectively invisible until he asked a man to move his feet.

Bad Eyes. The father and the man who'd introduced himself as Mountain Jack had a special bottle of whiskey. Despite this, Paxton's manner was extremely deferential to Bad Eyes and his father, only slightly less so to the man in buckskins.

"I feel like a man besieged," Bad Eyes complained to his father. "It was like this in Campore during the Mutiny. Damned wogs had us inside the compound for months. I believe our quarry has frozen himself. I haven't seen snow like this since I left Afghanistan."

"What makes you think so?" the older man inquired.

Bad Eyes tossed off his whiskey neat, poured himself another.

"You're right, you know. Man out there on horseback. Particularly a wounded man. We'll find him come spring thaw." Paxton laughed. "Buzzards will lead us right to the spot."

"We've been sure of our quarry before," the older man said, "and he eluded us. John Slocum is a clever and dangerous man. Smith-Dugdale leaves a widow and two children in Dorset."

The appearance of boredom was deceptive. Despite the nasal drawl and his appearance of contempt, it would be Lord Japhe, not his son, who would finally arrange some small pension for the family of the man who'd been killed in his service. It wouldn't be a unique expenditure. Any man who had served with Her Majesty's East India Company had seen his share of blood and, at times, only the thin red line of British troops had protected Lord Japhe's life. In the nature of things, men had died for him before, and the death of his personal secretary came as no shock—just an unpleasant loss.

Six months before, when they sailed from England, they'd been sailing for adventure. Not this sort of adventure.

The previous year, Little Will, Lord Japhe's son, had been discreetly cashiered from the Guards—allowed to resign. It wasn't his debts—God only knew how many times Lord Japhe had bailed Will out from under his creditors. It was something much worse. Little Will, Lieutenant Japhe, had beaten a man to death. The incident could be called an unfortunate consequence of routine punishment and, at Lord Japhe's urging, that was what Whitehall did call the matter. But they wanted to be shut of Lieutenant Japhe all the same.

So Lord Japhe put his affairs in the hands of his bailiff, closed the great manor house in Devonshire, and said, "Well, I think it's time we got to know each other. We've not been as close as father and son should be."

And now they were snowed in in some godforsaken outpost high in the Rockies, tracking a man who was likely dead, frozen in the terrible snow. The trip had started out better.

The American tour was a tradition among aristocratic Englishmen. After the experiences of Lord Stewart among the Indians and Mountain Men in Wyoming, the American

West became a popular visit for the wealthy and titled.

After three weeks at sea, their party landed at Manhattan—bustling, smoky, dangerous. When the Englishmen went on the town at night, they traveled armed, and Little Will carried a sword stick, too. They stayed in the Brevoort on Fifth Avenue, just a few short blocks from the theatrical entertainments.

Lord Japhe was more interested in the raw metropolis than his son, who liked the theater backstage, and was more fascinated by the dancers than the ballet.

Little Will was a womanizer. Well, thought Lord Japhe, it wasn't the worst thing to be, so long as ultimately he married properly. From what his father had seen, Little Will never let his affairs become love affairs.

Because of his previous position with the East India Company, Japhe was invited to luncheons and dinners with the speculators and merchants who thronged the narrow streets around Wall Street. Japhe dined with Quentin Roosevelt and Mr. Henry James, but couldn't arrange to meet Mr. Ralph Emerson, whose writings the nobleman had long admired.

After three days in the city, the two men automatically arranged their hours so that they never corresponded. When Little Will was sleeping—and Lord Japhe had to believe that some of the time Will actually *was* sleeping behind his closed bedroom door—why, then Lord Japhe was awake. And when Lord Japhe was being overcome by yawns, Little Will would be eager to take off for some champagne supper or dance hall.

Two weeks in New York and then west to Pittsburgh. Had they made their tour ten years before, perhaps they would have swung south to Atlanta, Richmond, or New Orleans, but these great cities had been so ravaged by the recent War they could provide no pleasant prospect for English tourists.

Pittsburgh reminded Lord Japhe of Birmingham. Little

Will found the music halls and saloons greatly inferior to New York's and used a cane on the skull of some impudent citizen who thought his manners were a touch too uppity for this democracy.

The young man was knocked unconscious. A human skull can be quite fragile, and everyone feared the worst until the young man recovered.

A formal apology from Lord Japhe to the young man's family—the boy was an engineer at Pittsburgh's mills, out for an evening on the town—and once more the Englishmen departed.

Little Will found St. Louis quite congenial and, for quite different reasons, so did his father.

Little Will found two saloons and one brothel that suited his fancies and resumed his nocturnal patterns.

Lord Japhe was fascinated by the town. St. Louis reminded the nobleman of the Calcutta market. It was so rushed, so full of diverse types of men. Riverboat pilots rubbed shoulders with flatboat skippers. An officer just returned from Fort Lincoln regaled his listeners with accounts of the Indian wars and great Indian leaders—Roman Nose, Crazy Horse, Black Kettle. Indians mingled with the crowds on the wharves. Many of them had followed the riverboats downstream, though there was a delegation of Comanche put up in the city's best hotel for a few days until the group would travel farther east seeking audience with the Great White Father.

Black men, red men, Chinese, whites. Fights were common in the riverfront taverns and the two Englishmen carried revolvers on their persons at all times. In St. Louis, Little Will found a gunsmith, Lederer, who outfitted them with suitable weapons for the western journey. He sold them Remington single-action revolvers: "I remind you, gentlemen, do not load the sixth chamber. Keep this chamber empty under the hammer. If you fall from your horse, or suffer some mishap, your revolver cannot fire." He sold them the Spencer rifles. "The very same rifles, gentlemen, issued to the U. S. Cavalry." They already had shotguns with their luggage.

Little Will provisioned their expedition and Lord Japhe was pleased to have him do it, because Little Will was spending too much time in that damn brothel.

James Smith-Dugdale, Lord Japhe's private secretary, joined them in St. Louis. The news he brought kept Japhe busy on the telegraph for several days. Thank God for the Atlantic Cable! Even at the outrageous price of twenty-five cents per word, at least he could communicate with his financial empire.

It was November when the three men left St. Louis, and snow was ready to fall. They took the riverboat north up the Missouri, steaming for weeks. One morning, somewhere in Dakota Territory, they woke to a world shrouded in white. It was quite beautiful.

Fort Benton, eight hundred river miles north of St. Louis, was the end of their passage. Lord Japhe took supper with Fort Benton's commander, one Major Reno, and was warned of some of the hazards of western travel. "It's one thing," Reno said, "to travel with an immigrant train of two or three hundred, all well armed. It's quite another for three men to venture through country the Sioux hold sacred." Reno added, "Good luck. I'm sorry to have missed your son."

Japhe's son was down by the riverbank where he'd found a young Indian whore and grunted his seed into her, lying on some filthy furs in a lodge that reeked of woodsmoke.

The Englishmen ignored Reno's warning and struck out to the south. Unconsciously, perhaps, Lord Japhe was hurrying their journey. Originally they'd planned to winter in St. Louis and make this more leisurely part of the tour in early spring. Now Lord Japhe wanted to hit south to the U.P. railroad before the snow got deep.

Though Lord Japhe was not a foolish or improvident man, he minimized the Major's warnings. He was a British financier traveling with his son, Lieutenant Will Japhe, late of the Guards, and his private secretary. The secretary, Mr. Smith-Dugdale, was a tousle-haired young man with great practical sense and a good hand for figures. Little Will treated him like a servant. Mr. Smith-Dugdale saddled their horses in the morning and checked the packsaddles. He cleaned the guns after an afternoon's hunt. He cooked lunch and dinner.

With a variety of guns, Little Will killed a hundred and six buffalo, seventeen mule deer, twelve antelope, and countless pigeons, swans, geese, and ducks. Mr. Smith-Dugdale kept a careful record of each kill, noting the details in a notebook he kept exclusively for that purpose. When the animal was unusually large he measured the head or horns and sometimes the length of leg with a dressmaker's cloth tape. He never remarked. He never hunted himself. He slept farthest from the fire, and the nights were getting very cold.

They connected with the Bozeman Trail and followed that broad path south, traveling right through the heart of the Crow and Lakota hunting grounds without seeing a single Indian. They regretted this very much, particularly Little Will, who had hoped to shoot one or two.

They stopped to spend two days at the Swan Ranch and stayed three months.

In the winter of 1867 an ox driver had been snowed in nearby. The snow caught him cold and hard, and fifty miles from shelter. He was an old hand and could take care of himself, but he turned his oxen loose to starve in the snow.

In the spring he returned expecting to find one or two starved survivors and found, to his delight, animals every bit as fat as when he'd left them. Throughout the winter they'd pawed down through the snow and found enough sweetgrass and bunchgrass to sustain them. They even put on weight.

It didn't take long for Texas cattlemen to figure that they could buy cheap range cows in Texas, drive them north, fatten them on northern grass, and ship them east on the railroad which was just then crawling toward the Rockies.

•

The three Englishmen rode into the headquarters of the Swan Ranch on December 17, 1868. The ranch owner was a business pal of Lord Japhe's and months ago had instructed his foreman to expect Japhe's party and afford them every courtesy.

Mountain Jack Elliot had been many things in his life: trapper, teamster, provost marshal for Sherman's Fifth Cavalry, and manager of five thousand acres and one thousand cows in the Wyoming wilderness. Swan Ranch had as much range as it had water holes and as many water holes as they could hold. They held against the Indians. They held against the small homesteaders following the railroad west. They held against rustlers. Four cowboys and the manager, Mountain Jack. Mountain Jack had never wanted to be an innkeeper or wet nurse for Englishmen.

The Englishmen were traveling too late in the season. It was only a hundred miles south to the U.P. railhead. It might as well have been ten thousand. The snow came.

Two cowboys stayed out in a line shack with the cows. Two others worked the home place, fixing saddles, mending the chuck wagon, getting ready for the spring.

The Englishmen and Mountain Jack played cards.

At first Jack's hospitality was unforced and cheerful. His boss's wish was his command. "Have another elk steak, Lord Japhe? Which one of you hombres want to try arm wrestling?" But as it snowed deeper and deeper, they took to drink and cards. Little Will stayed drunk from an hour before noon until he stumbled into bed and his father put away half a bottle of port every single day. Even the secretary, Smith-Dugdale, was losing his aplomb. Several times he'd barked back at Little Will's contemptuous orders. Sev-

eral times he'd taken Mountain Jack's part against the nobility.

They played poker, draw and stud. At the end of that
time, Little Will owned Mountain Jack's savings of $62.50,
his spare horse, and one old mining claim made out to him
by Bill Fairwether, who discovered the Virginia City Lode.
Since Mountain Jack set great store by that piece of paper,
Little Will liked winning it from him.

December rolled into January. In mid-February they had
a good, hard freeze and the two cowboys came in from the
line shack.

"We had some losses," one cowboy said.

"They was pretty peculiar," the other said.

They didn't say another word until whiskey opened them
up after dinner. They had seen mysterious tracks. "Shod
horses. No Indian ponies." The count of good cows kept
changing. "We counted nine hundred eighty one week and
next week it was seven seventy-five. Now we might have
missed a few cows back in the brush, but not two hundred
of them."

They speculated. Mountain Jack said the cows had wan-
dered off into some brushy draw.

For two weeks the word "rustler" wasn't mentioned,
though the word was in everyone's minds.

The Swan Ranch, like every other cattle outfit in the
country, had taken what it wanted by sheer force and nobody
even considered adjudicating matters. And, anyway, the
nearest judge was a hundred fifty miles away, on the far
side of the platte.

On the twenty-seventh of February Little Will said, "If
there are rustlers, it would be capital sport to go after them."

By then, Mountain Jack was so sick of his guests that
he agreed. Jack had once wintered with Big Ed Pollitz, who
was widely known as the least-bathed fur trapper in the
Crazy Woman Mountains. Even Big Ed's stink had been
easier to get used to than the young Englishman. The En-

glishman always held his words just a half-inch shy of the insult that would permit Jack to forget his duty and take his guest's life. Little Will never quite gave Jack direct provocation. Will was very good at that—baiting Jack, baiting him all the time.

"There's a couple long riders holed up thirty miles south of here," Jack said. "They got a soddy down past Poison Springs."

Little Will smiled. That evening he cleaned his Spencer rifle and his Remington revolvers, though Smith-Dugdale had done the job perfectly after their last hunt.

Mountain Jack reasoned, "Those two are the only white men nearby. Waco Billy and Pat Sorenson are wild ones. Both of them rode with the rebels during the war."

Rather to Lord Japhe's surprise, Billy and Pat were rustlers and had a hundred head of cattle penned in an enclosure behind their soddy. The soddy was in the middle of a broad valley, no way to hide it. And no way to hide the bawling cows, who'd already pawed through and eaten all the sweetgrass in this lot.

Six riders—Two cowboys, the English party, and Mountain Jack. Jack rode shoulder to shoulder with Will Japhe. Little Will's eyes sparkled and he had become quite amusing, recounting war stories from Afghanistan campaigns. And he didn't touch a drop of whiskey, not a drop.

Sometimes Mountain Jack wondered what Lord Japhe really thought of his son. Surely he must see. Surely he must know.

A thin curl of smoke came from the soddy chimney. The shuffle of the horses through the shallow snow, horse breath steaming in the chilly air.

"I count five horses," Jack said. "That one around back, you can just see his rump."

Little Will said, "I thought you said there were only two men."

"Could be pack horses."

Jack held a Henry rifle across his saddle bow. Somebody called the Henry a rifle "you loaded on Sunday and fired all week." Jack's finger was on the Henry's trigger and he wasn't wearing mittens. Mountain Jack said, "I'll bet they got long guns trained on us right now."

Little Will smiled. Will wore a proper business suit under his heavy sheepskin coat. He kept one arm inside the coat. "You Yanks don't know fear," Little Will said with a laugh.

They saw gunsmoke. Little Will cried out. They heard the report. Will had one hand clasped to his ear, which no longer was equipped with a lobe. The blood poured over his chilly knuckles.

A hollow voice came from the soddy. "Stop right there, Jack. I don't want you within pistol shot. Who's your pals?" The front door of the soddy kicked open and a small man stepped into the winter air. He had a rifle resting on his hip and a pistol stuck in the front of his pants. He was grinning. "What kin I do to help you?" he shouted.

"H'lo, Pat," Jack called. "Those our cows back there?"

"You noticed them? Ah, hell, Jack, we was hopin' you wouldn't notice them. I hope Waco Billy didn't hurt your pal too much. I bet Billy four bits he couldn't make that ear shot."

The riders spread out into a skirmish line facing Pat. Jack scratched the back of his skull with the front of his rifle. "If those are our cows, we're gonna hang you, Pat."

"I suppose there's no persuading you not to try."

"Likely some of us won't see the sunset," Mountain Jack rode forward casually.

Pat looked up at the sky. "I don't like the winter sunsets so much anyway," he said. "Just means that it's gonna get cold." He leveled his rifle and the skirmish line stopped in their tracks. "I guess that's close enough, Jack. I got something to discuss with you before we strike up the band."

The horses beside the soddy were restless. The winter plains were endless. "I ain't a patient man, Pat. But I won't snatch a man's last words."

Waco Billy came outside behind his pal. Billy was yawning hugely, like he'd just got out of bed. He just couldn't stop yawning.

"I got a pal of mine in the shack," Pat began.

Mountain Jack's horse stomped his feet nervously. Little Will Japhe eased his coat open and his pistol materialized, resting across his saddle horn.

"Naw, not Billy. Waco Billy's my ridin' partner. You hang me, you'll have to hang Billy, too."

Waco Billy grinned, like that was the best joke in the world. He was edging sideways toward the horses.

"You are tryin' my patience," Jack said. If Billy made a dash for those horses, Jack was going to drop him.

"My old Captain's inside. John Slocum's his name. He's just passin' through. He never knew nothin' about your cows."

"Pilgrim, step outside!" Jack shouted. A couple more of Billy's sly steps and things would go too far to be called back. Though he wore a heavy coat, the cold sweat was trickling down Jack's back.

The man who stood in the doorway kept his hands on the doorframes. His holstered revolver was draped around his shoulder out of harm's way. He was a tall, lanky gent, bigger than either Billy or Pat, and he was dressed better than them, too. His coat was a good wool and his Stetson was newly blocked. He stood like Samson holding up the pillars of the temple.

Billy continued, "John Slocum's just passing through. He ain't got no part of this. I knew him from the war."

Mountain Jack called out, "That the truth?"

The stranger said, "Not my quarrel, *amigo*. If you and Pat want to argue about cows, then you just go ahead. I'll just get on my horse and ride."

Jack knew Pat was speaking the truth. No man in his right mind would diminish forces just before a battle. The tall black-haired man spread his saddle blanket and saddled his horse. Good looking horse, big, like its rider. The rider was careful with his cinch strap and gentle setting the bit, like he had all the time in the world.

Little Will grew jittery at Mountain Jack's side. "You aren't going to let him ride out of here?"

"Pat's given me his word. He's a cow thief but he wouldn't lie. I'd rather take on two than three any day."

When he had everything to his satisfaction, the tall rider nudged his horse into a slow walk. He kept both hands high on the saddle where everybody could see he wasn't holding iron. "Pat, I reckon I won't be seein' you again this side of the River Jordan."

"I reckon not, John. Goodbye."

The dark-haired man nodded his farewell and put his boots into his horse, and that was when Little Will Japhe shot him.

The bullet took him high, heart or lung it looked like, and he slumped forward in his saddle. His horse jumped into a run. Pat's leveled rifle spoke and the sound past Jack's ear was like an angry bumblebee, snap and whine.

Little Will shot Pat. Jack could see the dust puff on Pat's chest.

Billy was running for the horses, leaving all the fighting for Pat.

The skirmish line rode on at the gallop. By now, others were firing, and poor gallant Pat didn't stand a chance. His rifle spoke again but bullets were plucking at his clothes and twitching his body and Pat's shots weren't aimed. He sank to his knees.

Little Will caught Waco Billy before he got his horse stretched out and backhanded the young man off the racing animal. Billy hit the ground hard, rolled a couple times, and when he got to his hands and knees he was eyeing half a dozen pistols. "Aw, shit," he said. "Aw, shit!" The tears weren't too far behind his eyes.

He was a young man, not yet twenty, and when they threw the rope over the roofbeam of the soddy and tied the other end to one of the cowboys' horses, he tried a joke.

"How many dead men you want for those blame cows?" he asked. His hands were lashed behind his back with pigging strings, so he just nodded at the body of the man who used to be his partner.

"Billy," Jack asked, "was it true what Pat said about that stranger? He wasn't with you boys?"

The boy's frightened eyes showed a spark of life. "You better have killed Slocum," he said. He licked his dry lips. "If you ain't killed him, he'll do for you like you did for Pat."

"And you," Jack said softly as he gave the nod.

The cowboy backed his horse and Billy lifted off the ground. The rope didn't break his neck so he kicked and jerked his legs and tried to get his feet on something to take the pressure off his neck. The cowboy snubbed the rope around an old watering trough. Billy was trying hard but his face was black and his eyes were bulging in their sockets.

Only Little Will watched the boy die, and he got up real near to do it.

In a soft voice, Jack gave his orders. The two cowboys were to stay in the soddy tonight, round up the cows, and push them back to the main herd if the weather stayed good. "If it snows again, just take your ease. I don't want you drivin' cows in bad weather."

Billy fouled himself and Little Will backed his horse a few feet.

"Mr. Japhe—" Jack rode up so his face was in the other man's face—"if you ever take a play away from me again like you did with Pat and that pilgrim, by God you'll not return home."

Little Will wasn't used to that kind of talk from anyone, let alone a rustic like Mountain Jack, but he held his tongue. He didn't say yes and he didn't say no. His pleasure in the hanging was ruined. When the four men rode out, Billy's life was very little, jerking away on a rope from his own ridgepole.

Mountain Jack rode in front. The bloodstains were good

and fast at first, great splashes on the snow. But they grew sparser, spots and then dribbles, and Jack knew the wound had closed right up. Slocum hadn't lost that much blood. They rode hard and fast into the snowy plains. The marks of Slocum's horse were clear as any marker. His pursuers could see tracks two and three hundred yards ahead. No horse could move faster than a canter. The snow was too slippery.

Lord Japhe rode beside Jack. Stiffly, Japhe said, "I apologize for my son."

Jack just gave him a look.

"Will was out of line," Lord Japhe added. "I am deeply sorry. If there's anything I can do to make amends..."

"Yeah," Jack snarled. "Keep a leash on him next time."

"What will we do now?"

"Now I'm gonna catch me a rustler and when I catch him, I mean to put an end to him."

"You don't believe what that man said?"

"Pat? Oh, hell, I knew Pat a long time. He wouldn't lie about a thing like that."

"Then the man we pursue..."

Jack gave a mean, hard grin. "Lord Japhe, your son's bullet just made that hombre a rustler. Because if he ain't a rustler then I'm a man who runs around shooting and hanging innocents. That's what the territory will believe. Either we caught a bunch of rustlers or we just strung up an innocent man. That's what'll be said out here. It's a hundred and fifty miles to the next white man, Lord Japhe. You got to keep your messages simple."

4

Late that evening, after the half-breed kid had finished swamping the joint and gone home; after Vinegar Varese had replaced his boss behind the long bar; after Lord Japhe and his son had gone off to their silent supper in the restaurant next door, Mountain Jack bought Sallie Arthur a drink and admired her openly. He said she was "a fine figure of a woman," and "maybe she wasn't no filly but she'd held onto her looks."

She eyed the black-bearded buckskinned man and wondered if maybe him and her could get a little something going. She let him buy her a drink. She listened to his brags—how he'd been a scout for Sherman, how he'd been the best buffalo getter the U. P. ever hired.

She said, "You look like a real hunk of man."

He beamed and tipped his hat. "Why, thank you Miss Sallie," he said. It had been in the fall that he'd seen his last white woman, and she was a horse-faced wife of an itinerant preacher who'd stopped at the Swan Ranch, lost, on their first mission to the Indians. They hadn't listened to Jack's warnings and he supposed they were dead by now, but that white woman had begun to seem mighty pretty to

73

him, that's how desperate he was. And now he was having drinks with this pink and gold and blue-eyed picture out of a dream. Jack was rough and crude, but Jack wasn't stupid. So he made the kinds of brags and boasts she'd heard before. He said things she'd likely known all along: how he was the manager of the great Swan Ranch with four winter cowhands working for him and better than a thousand cows.

"I got a nice room just upstairs and down the hall," Sallie said, tossing off her second whiskey like a trooper. "And I have some port wine I have been saving for a special occasion."

"I was thinkin' of havin' a little grub first," Jack said. "I ain't et under a roof in a week."

"Let's go have us a little wine," she said. "It's supposed to be good for the appetite."

So he hitched his collar and smiled and said, "Yes, ma'am," and followed her up the stairs and down the corridor. "I got a register in my room," she said. "It ain't so blame chilly."

The room was snug, redolent of perfume and powder. It was a woman's room and Mountain Jack hadn't taken off his hat and couldn't decide where to put it down.

"Just toss your hat and duds right there on that chair," Sallie said, drawing her curtains against the black night. "It's warm enough for you to take off your boots. Go ahead."

Mountain Jack blushed. "Ma'am, it's been a couple weeks since I had me a real bath."

Sallie cocked her eyebrow. "Maybe in the summertime with a line outside the door I'd throw you right out of here." She laughed.

"Well," he said, "it's just good, honest sweat." He pulled off his boots. His ankles were very white. His feet looked as tender as a baby's. His chest was dead white, though his face and neck were brown as shoe leather. He wore a little bag around his neck. "It's my medicine," he explained when he felt her eyes on it. "I was with the Indians for a good while."

"Well, you just take it off," she said. "I don't want no little bag filled with god-knows-what, rattlesnake rattles or lizard livers or cactus spines, bumping against my naked body. Why are you chasing that Slocum fella?"

Barefoot, bare-chested, but still in his buckskin pants, Mountain Jack took his ease in her upholstered chair and fired a havana. "I believe you heard downstairs, unless you was deaf. Slocum's a cattle rustler. You said you had some port wine." He chuckled. "I'm famished right now, but I hear it's good for the appetite."

She hadn't removed any of her clothes. She went to a chest for a decanter of wine and poured him a little glass. Decanter and wine glasses bespoke a certain gentility.

Between his huge thumb and forefinger, Jack took the eggshell-thin glass and tipped the wine down his throat.

She stepped out of her shoes. "I heard of a fellow name of John Slocum," she said.

"Black-haired fellow? Green eyes?"

"That's him. Rode with Quantrill during the War."

"A reb? Well, Pat was a reb. I knew that much of him."

"I don't know if John Slocum would have stolen another man's cattle. Maybe yes, maybe no. If he had, he wouldn't have ridden out on his pals like your John Slocum did."

"There was Swan cattle behind the soddy, plain as the nose on your face. Suppose you get out of that getup and we'll be both more comfortable," Jack suggested.

Her face changed slowly. "I ain't got anything against you," she said, her hand at the tie that fastened her dress together.

She shed the dress and there was more of her, all of her pink and sleek.

Her breasts were full and taut and uptilted. Her long blond hair cascaded over her breasts and the tiny pink nipples with the wide pale aureoles. "Do you like the port wine?" she asked.

Jack threw back his glass again, though it was already empty, and said, "Yeah, sure. It's fine."

She ran the pink tip of her tongue over her lower lip, and Jack's pants became painful. He shot one leg out, but that didn't give him much more comfort.

Below her belly button she sported a little belly and hair, more silver than blond, like a silver mink pelt.

"My, oh my," he said.

"You could get out of those breeches," she said. "You won't catch cold." She threw back the coverlet and her bed was fluffy and soft.

When he stepped out of his leather pants, his cock was so hard it hurt. He worried he might explode before he even got into bed with her. "I ain't been with a woman since August," he admitted, so she wouldn't think badly of him.

"I can see you're ready," she said. "Come on in here."

Her legs spread and her arms opened for him and when he lay on her and kissed her, he slipped up into her like butter, like after a long absence, he had come home.

"Just lie still," she murmured. "Just hold your butt still. Just put your mouth on my titty and let me do the work."

It wasn't very much work. She twitched inside once, twice, like she was giving Jack's cock a friendly squeeze.

He bucked up and jammed into her, seeking every crevice in her, flooding her with himself. The bottoms of his feet curled and he shot his seed.

She rubbed his shoulder. "My, ain't you the eager one."

He rolled onto his back and shielded his eyes with his arm. "Just like a damn kid," he said.

"Just means you're still healthy, Jack." She ran her hand through his chest hair. "We got time."

She put on a robe and poured two more glasses of the wine.

Before they made love, Jack wanted Sallie. Afterwards he began to like her. He thought she didn't have a mean bone in her body. "That Little Will Japhe," he said, "I'd stay clear of him if I was you."

"The son?"

"The same. He's got a wolverine streak in him some-where. He just plumb goes crazy when his blood is up."

She set the tiny glass within reach and hopped in beside him, still robed. "Do tell."

"It was Little Will who shot Slocum. Just up and fired, quick as a striking snake. Well, after we done for the others, we rode out after Slocum. There was Lord Japhe and his son and Smith-Dugdale, Lord Japhe's secretary. Now there was a straight shooter, that one. Had him a wife and kids back in England, too. Good man, wasn't afraid to get his hands dirty. We went after Slocum figuring to find him lyin' dead beside his horse before nightfall. We wasn't really equipped for no long chase. Well, the hoofprints kept on going due south, straight for Green River and the U.P. He'd lost a lot of blood and we were pressing hard as we could."

"You could put your hand on my breasts," she said. "Just kind of stroke while you're talking."

"That night it started to get dark and we holed up un-derneath some fir trees. Cut down some boughs and made lean-tos and ate cold pemmican for grub. Me and the Lord were godawful awkward talkin' after he made his apology for his son havin' such a hair trigger."

"Hair trigger? Mmmm. That's good."

"The fool shot too fast. Wasn't no need to shoot as fast as he did. Anyway, that night was awful bitter and about midnight there was northern lights, just bands and bands of light shimmering over the snow. I was awake to see them. Couldn't sleep a damn. Well, way we figured it, we'd find Slocum the next morning. Hurt man can't really build no shelter, and it was thirty or forty below. We'd find him froze where he stopped. He never stopped. In the morning we could see by the snow that'd drifted in his horse's tracks that he kept right on going, riding and then leading his horse. From the tracks we could see it hurt him every time he dismounted. His footsteps were somewhat crabbed, but he never stopped nor lit a fire.

"We was behind him then, for sure. I surely do like you holdin' me. I don't suppose I could interest you in puttin' your mouth on it? Ain't that fine. I'll just scootch up against the headboard so you got some room.

"He had the night's lead and his tracks went south straight as a die. Now I know that country about as well as any man alive. I trapped many of the creeks for beaver. That's right, just kind of tickle it with your tongue.

"I figured he would have lost the track somewhere but he was goin' due south by the directest way and we never had a chance to get around him. We rode all day, camped at night, and that night we didn't have no northern lights.

"Things wasn't any better with us. 'Pass the coffee.' 'I think my horse's got ice balling up in his hoof.' That's the sort of things we were sayin' to each other. I figured with the lead he got, he was gonna be in Green River a full half day ahead of us, and I was worried what kind of story he was going to tell. Turned out I didn't have to worry about that, because he never talked. He got his horse rubbed down and grained, made arrangements for the train, and bought himself some grub. He'd changed his shirt and though he walked a little funny, nobody in Green River knew he was shot. Naturally, everybody was curious about somebody riding in from the north, but he never said anything to any of them. He had two stiff drinks in the Buffalo Saloon and went down to the tracks to wait for the eleven fifty-three. He meant to go back East, and had bought a ticket to Omaha. Ouch! You be careful of those teeth. Just take it in your mouth and hold it still. There, that's better. That feels so good, honey, I wish it could go on forever.

"He would have got away with it, too, if the train had been on time. But snow had closed the track just thirty miles east of Green River and the eastbound didn't go out until the next day. This jasper Slocum was waiting at the station. He had his horse tied up at the hitch rail and his ticket in his pocket. He'd had a couple good looks along his back trail and must have known we was still after him. There was a constable in Green River and Slocum could have asked him for help, but he didn't. He waited there just calm as you please while the hours slipped by and the ticket agent said to us later that they'd a good chat and he never saw no sign that Slocum was hurt at all, just a pleasant soft-spoken kind of gent, that's what the ticket agent called him.

"Well, the eastbound wasn't leavin', but Slocum never seemed worried about a thing. He just said that since Omaha wasn't in the cards, maybe he'd see what the westbound had to offer. Well, the agent was surprised, but he changed Slocum's ticket and helped him to load his horse. Green River is a coal and water stop and the platform filled up with passengers planning to stretch their legs. There was gamblers and roustabouts and game hunters and soldiers all going out to end of track. There was a few ladies who wasn't no better than they should be. If you don't take your mouth off me, you'll be swallowin' some juice."

Her head came up, she wiped her mouth, and she smiled. "I don't expect you'll want to kiss me now," she said.

"Kissed you before, didn't I?" he grumbled. But his kiss was more a peck than a kiss as she snuggled onto his cock. He admired her breasts with both hands as she wiggled a mite.

"I'm gonna want a little longer ride than last time," she said as Jack continued his story.

"Slocum must have figured when we'd be riding in because he got on that train with the other passengers, calm as you please. When we rode into Green River, all we saw was the smoke. Next train would be that afternoon and wouldn't get through Cheyenne until next morning. I was for quittin' the chase. He'd outridden us and out-thought us, and him with a bullet in him that must be troubling considerable. But Lord Japhe's son wouldn't let well enough alone. Wiggle your butt. I like it when you wiggle your butt."

She arched back, her breasts above him like holds, her belly rippling. She ground him, she rocked him.

"Little Will tells his father we got to corral this Slocum because of what the story would do to his reputation in England. Me, I think he was just bullshitting the old man. His blood was up and he wanted to end the hunt with Slocum's scalp. Next morning, we followed. Slocum hadn't got off at Brewster Springs and he hadn't got off at Cheyenne. Little Will was hitting his flask, Lord Japhe was dictating to his secretary, and me, I looked out the windows. You know it's the devil of a job keeping the tracks open in the winter time, I don't know how . . . That's nice. Feels so good when you lean back like that."

Through gritted teeth, she said, "If you was to hump a little instead of yakking, that'd please me."

So he grabbed her hips and ground up into her until her belly went flat, plumped out, went flat again. "Oh," she said. "Oh . . ."

He said, "Jesus Christ, I can't hold 'er now!" and filled her with himself.

He rolled off, just lay flat on his back staring at the pressed tin ceiling. His cock felt awful cold and he grabbed the edge of a blanket to cover himself.

She was panting, too. Finally she said, "That was nice. Trouble with the winter up here, you see the same gents all the time, regular as clockwork. There's Johnson on Thursdays, Paxton on Wednesday afternoons for the rent. Major Devers when he's in town. Same faces, same flesh. Gets kind of boring."

"Not so boring as being alone," he said. "You want one of my havanas?"

"Sure." She laughed. "It's okay for me to smoke. I'm a fallen woman."

He touched her breasts. "Haven't fallen too far, if I'm any judge," he said.

"Let me pull this cover over us. You can put the ashtray on your stomach."

They smoked their havanas—him savoring it, her more experimentally—while he talked of how they'd happened to follow a man deep into the Wind River Mountains in February.

Point of Rocks, end of track, wasn't a boom town, but it was gearing up for the job. When railroad work started in March, the town wanted to be ready. A couple hundred tinhorns, as many whores and half that many holdup men, road agents, and roughnecks had already gathered. With no railroad men yet to rob they robbed each other. Point of Rocks was a convenient jumping-off point for the last half of the Oregon Trail and the edge of town was an enormous immigrant camp. From time to time one of these immigrants strolled into town and was plucked quicker than a Christmas goose. But generally they stayed clear of the gamblers and girls who, of necessity, fed on each other.

Those few months toward the tag end of winter found more scrupulously honest card games in Point of Rocks than before or since. Nobody wanted to be accused. Snowed in, tempers were short and the merest hint of cheating buried a man.

As he told his story, Mountain Jack smoked his cigar and sipped his port wine and wriggled his toes in this fine woman's perfumed bed. "It's a dangerous town, all right," he said. "Just full of poisonous varmints and bulls of the herd. Every day a man died with his boots on. I never fancied that myself. I always figured to live long and go out in style with somebody weeping at me from the end of a big old bed. Bare feet. It's fine for a young daring man to want to die with his boots on, but me, I'd have 'em off, just like this."

"So," she said, "Slocum was in Point of Rocks."

"Oh, hell, yes. He wasn't no trouble at all to find. I guess he thought he was done runnin'. And maybe if he'd been in some halfway civilized town, with sheriffs and judges and the like, he would have been."

The English bunch asked loafers on the station platform

and several of them had noted the tall, dark-haired rider with the ash-pale face. "I thought he had the consumption," one man said.

The whole area was enjoying a chinook. The warm southern wind had melted a considerable amount of snow, and the engineers were out with maps and core samples just in case this was really spring and they could get on with their work. The sun was warm on the four men's backs as they rode through the tent city seeking John Slocum.

Mountain Jack recognized his horse, tired and hipshot, outside one of the larger tents that served as a grog shop and saloon.

"You got a weapon, Mr. Smith-Dugdale?"

"Yes, sir." And the English private secretary extracted an Allen pepperbox from his coat pocket.

"If he gets by us, you wait until he's right on top of you before you fire. Then touch her off."

"Yes, sir, I surely will." The secretary replaced his hand in his coat pocket and wore a look of the greatest resolution.

Mountain Jack sent Little Will around back, "Since back-shootin's your specialty," he said. Mountain Jack was heartily sick of the cruel Englishman.

The black-haired rider sat alone at a table in the back. He'd bought himself a bottle of rye whiskey. His glass was on the table before him. His face was full of pain.

He spotted them right away but didn't move a muscle as they threaded their way through the other drinkers toward their quarry.

Some men lay against the side wall of the tent, pockets ripped out, drunk to insensibility. Some men leaned and one knelt against the barrels that served as a bar. The air was rich with booze stink and tobacco stink.

Both Slocum's hands were around his whiskey glass. His eyes were green, a funny kind of green. They could see that now they'd come closer. He didn't sit like he was hurt but his voice was throaty and slow. "I hope you ain't plannin' to throw a party," he said.

"You got guts, I'll give you that," Mountain Jack said. "Why don't you and us step outside? We got business to discuss."

He sat ever so still. In that same raspy voice he said, "I ain't no rustler. I dream about the men I killed. I don't want you in my dreams."

"Well, I don't suppose you got any choice..." That's what Mountain Jack said just as all hell broke loose. Mountain Jack had expected trouble, he was primed for trouble, and he had one hand on his pistol butt. But Slocum's table crashed into his knees so hard Jack folded over it. Slocum was wounded but he had strength to spare. That table came up like it was steam-driven, and Mountain Jack just flipped over it and, quick as that, John Slocum laid a pistol next to his ear.

Little Will Japhe came through the back of the tent, quick as a rattlesnake. He had a Greener in his hand, an eight-gauge.

The drinkers started to scramble. Some whooped through the front door, some hit the ground, some dropped behind the barrel bar, others took a drink—maybe their last drink—and watched calmly.

The muzzle of John Slocum's Colt was pressed against Lord Japhe's left eye. He was pressing pretty hard, too, because tears were running out of the Englishman's other eye and his mouth was making some odd motions. "You take another step and I'll kill your pard," Slocum said in that slow, pained way of his.

"My father is Lord Japhe, Earl of Devonshire," Little Will said. Both hammers were cocked and he was leaned into the Greener like he anticipated a recoil.

"You gonna be the lord when he's dead?" Slocum asked conversationally.

Little Will stepped sideways. If he got any closer, his pattern would shrink. It'd get hotter but smaller. "Yes."

"Well, then." Slocum's smile hurt his face but his eyes were laughing. "If you mean to kill me, you better be mighty sure. Because I'll put one in you soon as you touch her off. I can't say where it's gonna be. Hell, maybe I'll just bust your ankle. If you're a gambling man, it might be a good wager. You get to be a lord of somewhere and lose an ankle or a thumb. Course, I'll be *attemptin'* for your balls."

Behind a goosegun that could have killed half the men in the room, Little Will looked into the eyes and laugh of the man facing him and dropped that Greener so fast it smoked. Little Will shot his hands up over his head pretty quick, too.

A couple of the gents who were close to John Slocum and would have been hit when Little Will touched off his scattergun wiped their brows or gritted their chattering teeth until they could bite into another glass of their favorite poison.

John Slocum lowered his Colt. He said, "Next time I see you, it'll mean your death," and strolled out of that booze tent like he owned it.

It was over. And lucky nobody else had died. That was what Lord Japhe was thinking. He was also wondering why God had cursed him with such a son. He was also hoping that cold mark on his eyeball would fade and he was looking through a veil of tears. Everybody quite forgot Smith-Dugdale, the loyal secretary.

Smith-Dugdale waited outside, just as he'd been told, and kept his hand jammed into his pocket gripping the bird's-foot butt of the pepperbox.

Eight little .26 caliber barrels touched off with a single trigger. It was a drummer's weapon, a preacher's weapon, a weapon for a woman. Smith-Dugdale didn't know that. He'd been told to wait. He had a wife and family to feed.

The sudden silence inside the tent cued him. He'd hardly got settled behind the near wheel of somebody's goods wagon, hardly leveled his nervous pepperbox when John Slocum came out and mounted his horse.

"You, sir!"

Those were James Smith-Dugdale's last words. Slocum's first bullet smashed through his throat, the second broke his left elbow. He felt nothing at first—a gagging sensation, the knock against his left elbow. He tugged the trigger and eight wild slugs blasted at John Slocum.

The secretary felt pain dulled by the throb of the blood rushing from his ruined jugular. His brain went dim. He tried to summon up a remembrance of his wife and children as he toppled against the wagon and slipped backward into the slush, but he could not find his loved ones in his memory before he died.

One freak slug clipped the edge of John Slocum's pistol butt, just touched it and jolted the weapon out of his hand.

The other slugs buzzed past. Most of them threw high. One misloaded slug went low and smacked into Slocum's horse and started him crow-hopping down the street.

Slocum was doing his clean best to hang on when Little Will stepped out of the tent and lifted the scattergun to his shoulder and boomed.

Seventy-five yards down the slushy street, the shotgun balls didn't hurt John Slocum, but they bruised his pride. One-handed, he pulled his horse around. He hauled so hard on the reins that the animal went down to his haunches making the turn. John Slocum came up in the saddle and had his Sharps rifle at his shoulder, the big fifty the buffalo hunters called that Sharps, but his tormented chest wound broke loose again and he said "Oh" and the Sharps fell from his nerveless hands into the street where, later, Mountain Jack claimed it.

Slocum's horse turned again and galloped out of Point of Rocks on the only road there was.

The road was open, the old immigrant road. Skirting snowbanks, Slocum's horse took off, running pretty hard in full, warm sunlight.

So now Lord Japhe had a dead secretary. He'd wanted to let this thing go. He'd been ready to put his foot down.

Too late for that now. Smith-Dugdale perished—most unfortunate. "Jack," Lord Japhe said quietly, "him or us."

Mountain Jack looked at the body of the little man he'd come to like. Lord Japhe's secretary lay immersed in street slush.

"Slocum's wounded," Little Will said. "I wounded his horse. There was blood right here." He touched the place on his own rib cage where he'd seen the bright red blood.

"We leave right away," Lord Japhe said.

"First we bury our dead," Mountain Jack said.

5

While Lord Japhe ate dinner at William Paxton's Inn and Mountain Jack lay comfortable in Sallie Arthur's arms, Lacey Tripp was trudging back to the dugout.

The snow had started again as he made his way home. Snow that covered all misdeeds, every track. It fell in a solid, quiet, swirling wall to blanket the planet as the boy sludged back along the ridgelines, favoring his old snow-shoes as much as he could.

He'd done his work, sweeping and cleaning and Jessica's work, too. Paxton had insisted that the boy tidy his bedroom and fill his water jug. Lacey had done as he was told and spat into the water jug. Lacey hoped he had some sickness in his spittle that would make Paxton sick as a dog. Maybe Lacey's spittle would change Paxton into a half-breed. How ambitious would Paxton be as a scorned half-breed? Would Paxton shelter anyone from Little Will's evil eyes?

Little Will's eyes were the deciding factor. The boy simply couldn't envision their helpless guest under the baleful glance of those eyes. He'd stuttered and fallen silent and swallowed the story he'd been meaning to tell. Kept it swallowed, too, though there were times that day, asking

some stranger to lift his feet so he could sweep, emptying
the overflowing brass spittoons, that the secret trembled on
the tip of his tongue.

Five hundred dollars. My, my. And Captain Slocum
would probably die anyway.

And if he didn't Lord Japhe's bunch would find him as
soon as the weather improved. They had snowshoes in town,
too, and those who knew how to use them. When the weather
broke they'd start up their search. Looking for a wounded
man on a wounded horse tracked to within five miles of
here and headed right up the gulches, by God. Even the
most pacific miners were pretty bored after a long winter
snowbound and would welcome the chance to join the pursuit. Besides, who couldn't use five hundred cartwheels?

Well, they wouldn't start tonight. Lacey Tripp had one
night to prepare for the searchers, and already he knew what
he must do. He didn't think any more about the right and
wrong of it. It never occurred to him that what he was doing
might be dangerous to him or to his sister.

Once again the weary boy reached the warmth of home
just before darkness. Ten minutes later he would have
watched his landmarks disappear, change in the heavy snow.

The cabin was warm, almost too warm, a blast of heat
that crystallized the snow standing on his shoulders and hat
brim. Smell of broth cooking.

Captain Slocum lay stark naked on a cot in the farthest
corner of the dugout, tossing on the cot.

Jessica hugged her brother. "Where is our help?" she
asked. "Every hour I've expected someone to come. I was
afraid something had happened to you."

"Him," Lacey pointed at the figure on the cot. "This
John Slocum. They say he is an escaped rustler and a murderer, too."

"He opened his eyes," she said. "He is so hot. He's
burning up with fever. Who says this of him? Who says he
has murdered?"

There was genuine shock in Jessica's eyes. That this stranger, this near-infant she had saved, could be a murderer was quite beyond her comprehension. She knew this man. He had become like her own little baby.

"Couple bad hats in South Pass." Lacey poured himself a cup of broth and blew on it before he took a cautious sip. He told Jessica what he'd learned that day. He said, "If anybody's a murderer, it's that Little Will. Lookin' into his eyes is like lookin' into the pits of hell."

"I thought you wasn't a Christian," she said. "Captain John opened his eyes today. He's got green eyes, Lacey, prettiest green eyes you ever seen. Oh, they're all bloodshot and the whites are more yellow than white, but his eyes are really pretty. He didn't see me. I guess he didn't know where he was. He licked his lips and I guess he said a word but I can't guess what it was, more like a crow's caw than human speech. I been bathin' him when he gets hot and then, when he gets cold again, I skid him back near the stove. I been keepin' it so hot on account of him. I believe we're gonna burn some furniture here tonight. Lacey, I'm afraid he's gonna die. Come over here and feel 'round this bullet wound. The hot part is spreadin' down his chest and toward his throat. I fear he's a goner, Lacey—and we tried so hard."

Briefly, she wept on her younger brother's shoulder and rubbed her eyes dry with a towel that still bore the imprint for "Wetzel Seed—They grow right." "That feels better. I'm a woman, you know, and sometimes I just got to cry."

Since Lacey hadn't seen their guest since late morning, the red splotch of extended infection alarmed him.

Softly she said, "Lacey we're gonna have to cut out the bullet."

He didn't answer right away, just looked at Captain John. Damn, the man had been hard used.

"If we kill him, we won't be hurrying things much," he observed. "You ever see anybody cut out a bullet?"

She'd only heard talk of it. "Wound's supposed to be clean," she said. "And the knife sharp. And all the poison drains out and you sear it with a red-hot poker."

Lacey was amazed at this final detail. "If that won't kill him, nothing will," he observed.

"Will you do that part? I suppose I could do the cutting if you was to lie across him and hold him down."

"We'll tie his arms down. That way he won't get away from us. He probably won't wake up anyway."

Wrong guess. At first when Jessica broke the skin of the bullet wound, he paid no attention, but as the pressure got heavier he flinched and as the knife scoured around the ball above his breastbone, he lurched against the laces that held him against the cot, and Lacey had to flop across him and pin him still.

When he lunged, Jessica let the knife slip deeper into his body. The knife wobbled in his chest, the point just beneath the ball. Jessica felt faint, but her hand was steady.

Slocum flopped back from his convulsion. He groaned. His teeth chattered. Jessica had started this business and she wasn't about to stop until she completed it. She ignored the sounds from his teeth, stuck the knife into a new point, slipped under the ball, and scooped the ball in a semicircle of flesh.

A gout, a stench, as the wound exploded. Must have been a pint of pus in the flesh, irritation and infestation.

The cabin smelled very bad. Lacey said, "I'm gonna get up off him now. He's out, and I think I'm gonna puke."

"You just stay there, Lacey Tripp. If I can cut him, you can do your part and hold him down." With the heels of her hands she pressed against the edges of the hole she had dug and forced pus out until the fluid ran nearly clear except for the faint pinkness of new blood.

"Will you hurry it up?" Lacey said. "He's startin' to toss and turn now."

The cot legs rattled on the floor as the bound man heaved against his bonds.

"It'll be just a second." She set the tip of her brother's razor sharp Barlow against the proud flesh covering the bullet's track and opened his skin like a butcher boning a roast. Her stroke was so swift that the knife work was done before the wounded man tossed against the pain.

Jessica felt a little woozy herself. The fluid she'd released from the wound track did nothing to make her stomach lie easier. "Bring that stove poker," she said.

"It'll plumb kill him," her brother objected. "Listen to his breath a-rattlin'. Touch him with a poker and it'll just rattle right on out of his body, and that'll be the end of him."

Rather gratefully, she agreed. They washed Slocum's wound with the whiskey from his flask and bound it with the cut-off leg from his clean long johns.

Slocum's chest rose and fell, interrupted by an infrequent, shuddering sob. Jessica Tripp laid her ear to his chest and listened. "If he takes the pneumonia now, he's done," she announced.

"Kill or cure," her brother said gloomily. "How 'bout some more of that horsemeat broth?"

As they drank the strong, nourishing broth, he told her what he thought tomorrow would bring. "Snow or no snow," he said, "There's gonna be riders out after him. Five hundred dollars is money to bring any man out into the snow."

"They wouldn't dare just burst right in here."

He looked at their guest covered with their best coverlets right next to the stove. "You think he'll live until tomorrow? If he was to die, we could turn his body in for the reward and, besides, that four thousand in gold would belong to us, too. Nobody needs to know about that."

"He's gonna live," Jessica said in a tone that cut short all speculation. Captain Slocum was hers, and she meant to nurse him back to health, not turn him over to the first bunch of hooligans who knocked at her door. "You'll have to get rid of the horse," she said.

"What?"

"Anybody coming up on our house is gonna see it. It's plain to see and the snow won't completely cover it. You're just gonna have to get it away."

"How can I do that?"

"You're the man," she said smugly, delivering an honor he'd always coveted but never thought to be onerous.

It snowed all night. In the middle of the darkness, when Lacey rose to check their guest, they were completely out of firewood, and he fed the stove chair legs to keep it going. There was enough gold in the Captain's pocket to buy every chair between here and California.

The Captain was breathing easier and his chest wasn't hot at all. Maybe draining and cleaning his wound had done some good. Even though they'd lose the gold, Lacey hoped so. He listened for the Captain's breath, gentle as the beat of moth wings, and felt himself fragile. If a strong man like this could be brought down, what hope was there for a stripling of twelve years?

In the morning, Jessica fried more horsemeat, and Lacey ate until his stomach couldn't accept any more. The more horse inside him, the less he'd have to drag away from the cabin.

Captain Slocum's breathing was pretty good and he had no fever to speak of. None of the rattling in the lungs that meant pneumonia. At any moment he might open his eyes, and Lacey wanted to be there when that happened. But Jessica broke up the rest of the chair and shooed him out into the weather.

The horse was a ragged chunk of meat, maybe a ton of it. Lacey looked at the mound of dead meat with dismay.

In South Pass the search was being mounted with dispatch and efficiency. Men with snowshoes gathered in groups on the street. They all went armed, because Little Will Japhe had warned them that they pursued an extremely dangerous quarry.

Lord Japhe took a leisurely breakfast in Paxton's dining room. If snowshoes enabled a search near South Pass, couldn't they serve to take himself and his son and Mountain Jack out of here?

Not likely. That was William Paxton's opinion. "So long as you stay close to shelter," Paxton said, "you'll be all right. But if you got out there in the rough country and a real norther came down, you wouldn't last the night."

"I see."

"How do you like your breakfast?"

"Acceptable." Lord Japhe cut off further conversation.

A few persuasive men argued that John Slocum might have made it as far west as Miner's Delight. The largest armed party, led by Vinegar Varese, struck out for that operation. Five miles away as the crow flies, but an eternity for men crashing through the thin crust of the snow, breaking their rawhide bindings, stumbling into drifts.

Three parties went out: to South Pass, to Atlantic City, and to Miner's Delight. The South Pass group got quite lost in the falling snow and found themselves with no alternative but to return to home base.

While they crashed around looking for landmarks, Lacey Tripp was cutting pine poles. He picked skinny trees, bent by the snow, and by cutting them at the bend, created runners. He lashed shorter poles across the runners. He lashed a drawbar to the runner tips so they wouldn't turn in their bindings and flop apart. It had taken him the better part of the morning. It was crude and quite heavy, and very clumsy. But it was a sled, and he hoped it would haul the horse.

Lacey' spirits were slightly lifted by the ease he felt and the good warm broth in his belly. They weren't going to haul *all* of it away, no sirree. They'd keep the loin and one ham anyway. Meat was meat, and if anybody inspected their larder, they could claim the meat came from a bear.

Humming, he shoveled a space clear along the horse's

backside so he could work. Six inches of snow covered the horse's hide, his wound, the gap where Lacey had cut earlier, his ice-glazed eyes.

The South Pass group returned to town before noon. They were quite downhearted and walked with the heavy gait of exhausted men.

Little Will Japhe met the men at the door of Paxton's hotel, dry-footed on the bare wooden porch. With the snow clinging to their coats and hats, they looked like a flock of sodden, hungry sheep. Their eyes were lowered.

"South Pass?" Little Will cried. "Did he cross at South Pass?"

"Dunno," one worthy grumbled. "Didn't see no sign of him."

"How far did you go?"

They didn't know that, either. The miners were cold and weary, but something in Little Will's posture held them there on that uncomfortable place as he fired a long havana. "In India, we had niggers to do the hard work," he explained once a few puffs had set his cigar glowing. "Of course, they gave up easier than white men did. That's why we were able to conquer India, don't you see, because the niggers would fight hard, but then they'd give up." He went on in that vein for a few minutes. None of what he said sat too well with his listeners.

"Can't find a damn thing out there," one miner complained.

"You see that snow? It's coverin' everything."

"Likely he's dead. Likely he's froze to death."

Little Will cracked a smile. He upped the ante. "A thousand dollars to the man who brings him in," he said. "Dead or alive."

That put a different light on things, a rosier sort of light. Those men who had clean, dry clothes went home to change into them and all partook of the elk stew at Paxton's. "On the house, gentlemen. On the house." Nourished and warmed, they donned their snowshoes again and shuffled out of town toward Camp Stambaugh. Perhaps John Slocum had bypassed South Pass altogether during that chinook, just a few days ago—was it that long?—and found refuge with the pony soldiers. If so, they'd blast him out of there.

Since everybody able-bodied was searching in the storm and since the half-breeds hadn't come in, William Paxton was doing swamper's work and vowing to fire those kids as soon as he found replacements willing to accept wages he personally considered munificent.

His employees were, at that minute, busy chopping up a dead horse. Since the crosscut saw made no very great impression on the frozen animal, Lacey Tripp swung a double-bit chopping axe at the hide and flesh and bone. The axe worked well enough. Each chop sent splinters of frozen horse flying and penetrated the carcass another inch or so. Half a dozen overhead swings and Lacey traded off with his sister, who managed a dozen good whacks of her own. The meat closed slightly between blows and it was very difficult even for good axemen to plant the edge in the same spot each swing. They cut through a quarter-inch of hide, through the fat, which broke up in chunks, through muscle and bone. With the exception of the fat, the cutting was uniformly difficult, frozen flesh being no softer than frozen bone.

Lacey managed to separate the head and neck from the body and cut through the ribs where he'd already severed the spine for food. They managed to roll everything but the head onto the makeshift sled. Lacey threw himself into the harness. It moved very slowly.

"I can't come with you, Lacey," Jessica said. "I got to watch after the Captain. Just take it away and toss it down a prospect hole."

Rear legs caught in the snow and half pulled the horse off the sleigh. The boy looked unhappily at his load. "If I don't cut them shanks off that animal, it's gonna hang up every hundred yards."

"Try the saw, Lacey. With the saw we can cut them off."

• • •

While the two struggled with their saw, Little Will was telling his father that the search party was "no better'n niggers. A touch of the whip, that's what they need if they're ever to do the work of white men."

His father sat at the best table in Paxton's saloon. A bottle of the finest Highland malt was open before him. He'd not touched the glass he'd poured nor the coffee, cold in the cup beside it. Lord Japhe wore a gray business suit.

His son wore black. He'd adapted to the American West to the extent of wearing pistols gunslinger style in open-topped holsters. He thought the practice amusing and hoped to learn and practice the American quick draw. He tossed off a healthy slug of whiskey. "I sent the lazy bastards back out there," he said.

"It hasn't worked," his father said.

"What hasn't worked? We'll find this Slocum yet."

"I believe this winter has made us murderers," Lord Japhe said slowly. The words pained him.

His son laughed quite heartily.

In the soft snow, Lacey found it hard going. Even with the horse's hooves removed and tucked under the carcass so it wouldn't roll, towing that sled was all his strength could bear. He meant to get the horse up one slope and down the other side.

The rate the snow was falling, every trace would be covered in an hour or so. He wanted to stay below the Atlantic City trail.

On that slope he was thankful for the soft snow, because at least the sled didn't slide sideways too much.

Under the low ceiling of the falling snow, on a ridge sparsely poled with dark green jack pine, just below the ridge top, a young half-breed was pulling a sled containing much of the mortal remains of a horse.

Though the boy wore a full sheepskin jacket and had some rags tucked under the two pull straps to ease the pain, the straps were cutting him. At first they hurt like hell but that earlier pain had given way to numbness. That numbness only vanished when the pull was unusual—when, say, the sled slipped a foot or so sideways and the straps wrenched one of his muscles. Then the boy cried aloud. Why not? There were none to hear him, and the falling snow muffled his complaint.

Lord Japhe downed his malt whiskey with a single toss and the eyes he fastened on his son and heir were not kind. "When we return home," he said, "I shall bestow a settlement upon you so you shall not want."

His son's quick smile was charming but slightly puzzled. "You mean to increase my allowance? That's very kind. Ten thousand a year leaves me with my pockets unmercifully thin, don't you know."

"A single bulk settlement in lieu of the estate," Lord Japhe said in an emotionless voice.

On top of the ridge Lacey took a short breather. The off slope was no worse than the one he'd so painfully traversed, and below was the gully where he hoped to shed much of his load.

The weight was so oppressive, so nearly his match at every step, he'd come to think of the burden as almost alive. "You and me, horse," he said, "we're gonna go on to the bottom of this slope, and that's where I'm gonna leave your big ass. Come on now, horse, give!" He threw himself into the traces to break his runners' frozen grip. The sled came away too easy and, for a moment, he was lost in the traces. The heavy end of the sled came around on the ridgetop. It had been partially blown clear and the snow was shallower and the ice underneath harder and more slippery. Lacey's terrific jerk sawed the back end around to him and the slope's fall line. For a second the sled tipped, jerking up on Lacey's harness. "God damn it!" he cried as the sled started down the slope backward. It jerked him right off his feet and he banged and bobbed along behind the sled as it picked up speed. His mouth was full of snow. His eyes saw through a white fur on his eyebrows.

The sled runners rode on the old crust until they hit a soft spot in that crust and broke through. The snow built up against the sled.

Lacey gave up completely. He lay passive as a sea anchor and when finally, on its own, the sled halted, he was slow to get to his feet. Lacey had snow down his neck and inside his pants. He scooped snow from his pants. His rope belt had broken. He spliced the broken ends together.

As his numb fingers worked, snow fell all around him. The boy in the twisted makeshift harness with his load of dead horse—all were covered with the sweetest, most gentle snow.

Lord Japhe took leave of his son once he had made known his startling decision. Now he sat upstairs and wondered at how his son had taken the news. At first Will's face had blackened at the news that he would receive only a portion of what he had come to regard as inevitably his: the lands, the securities, the whole of Lord Japhe's estate. But the blackness flitted off his face light as a hummingbird. "Your wish, Father," he said formally.

When Lacey got his fingers back into his mittens they were already blue with cold.

The sled had careened halfway down the slope and the back end was burdened with broken snow, and still more snow came. Although there was no human near enough to see him, the boy wouldn't let himself cry. He set himself, instead, to scooping the extra snow off the back of his sled and twisting it down hill.

Naturally, as if to deliberately aggravate him, it slid a few feet and stopped. The boy took up the traces again and tugged and the sled came away, tugged, and came away again. Though he never quite could get it to travel loose on its own, it did get loose enough to bust him in the ankles. He'd tug, get smacked in the tendons, and that would stop the sled, so he'd tug again.

At the bottom of the gully he toppled the ass end of the horse off the sled into the deepest part of the gully. It sank through the soft snow and he pushed snow over it with his arms.

The tracks were a mess, but the fresh snow would cover them. Now all he had to do was climb the next ridge.

6

When John Slocum opened his eyes, he felt a great lassitude.

The glow on his cheek—was it the glow of a stove?

He tried to think.

Somewhere near someone was singing. A woman's voice? A child's voice? The voice sang, "I hunt the deer, the long-legged deer, and I will wear its skin!" Slocum knew the song from somewhere. It was, he thought, a Crow song.

Crow? Where was he? Overhead, poles served as rough rafters and rough-sawed wide pine planks were roofer planks.

He could move his head but he chose not to. He sent feelers up and down his body checking for damage. Legs okay, hands, arms okay, pressure in his chest. Maybe he was shot there.

He wondered at that. Wondered who'd got him. Some yank? No, that was years ago. John Wesley Hardin? No, he'd ridden out of Texas and Hardin was in the Texas state pen. Weak as a baby, but his eyes open, John Slocum reviewed his life, seeking information about where he might be and how he'd gotten into such trouble.

Remounts. He'd brought remounts up the trail to Fort Bozeman in October, that much he remembered. The trail was awful damn dangerous, passing right through the heart of Sioux country, but the Army was paying top dollar for bay horses, geldings and mares and John Slocum had trailed forty of them north to Fort Bozeman. He intended to stay the winter in the fort.

The woman or child stopped singing. Slocum heard her soft footfalls. Her face swam into his vision, bent down to his, full of concern. "You awake, Captain? You recovered your wits?"

He meant to say yes, he had, but his voice box was rusty and his assurance came out as a croak.

The smile washed all the weariness off her face. "Well, I'll be. I believe you're gonna live after all. I thought you was on the other side, for sure. Gone away and gone to stay. Good to hear your voice, Captain, though you don't make no more sense than a rusty hinge."

He licked his lips and whispered, "Where am I? Who?"

"Well, I'm Miss Jessica Tripp. Miss Jessica Tripp." She pointed a delighted finger at her own chest. "And you are in a dugout house owned by me and my brother, Lacey. It was left to us by our mother. She's dead."

God damn, he was weak. He had no strength left for the questions he wanted to ask. He smiled; he closed his eyes to drift off again. He part woke when she propped him up and he definitely woke when she touched his lips with a hot spoon. His eyes blinked open.

"Now you just take some of this broth. You got to get your strength back, Captain."

His eyes looked the question.

"Yes, you bet. We been feedin' you like this ever since your horse started rubbin' on our house. That'd be three days now. Lacey's out there hiding your horse because there are some hard men riding after you and they mustn't know where you are."

Slocum concentrated on swallowing the broth. She clinked the spoon against his teeth. He kept his eyes closed. He felt nourishment spreading through his body like new warmth. He'd been hurt before, but he couldn't recall any time when he'd been quite this helpless. He had enough strength to lift his arm from the bed covers, but could only let it flop again.

He had a strong mental picture of the man who'd shot him. Slocum had been riding away from trouble, not seeking it, and the dude with the sneak gun had caught him with a slug that knocked the air right out of him and then his vision. Bullet had taken him in the chest. That was the wound.

"You're gonna get well," she said. And she sang her Crow song again. Slocum remembered that it was one of the songs Indian mothers used as a lullaby, and a tiny grin crinkled his cheeks.

"Now, don't you get to laughing at me," she scolded happily. "Just drink this broth. It's the last thing that horse of yours will ever do for you."

And John Slocum had another mental image. An image of riding into the heart of a snowstorm, wounded, on a wounded horse, singing his own death song.

Sometimes things that start out all right just keep on turning worse.

He'd got a good price from the Army, a hundred dollars a head. They would have given him a hundred and fifty for his big Appaloosa stallion, because the Colonel at Fort Bozeman had his eye on it. Slocum had taken a liking to the horse and wouldn't sell.

Well, the unsold horse didn't matter so very much in November when the snow began to fly and John Slocum was holed up in Fort Bozeman expecting a quiet winter. A little poker, purely for recreation.

But the Colonel still wanted Slocum's horse. Slocum could see him now, a florid man with drinker's veins on the end of his beaky nose.

Slocum kept the games small until January. During the long stretches when the weather was too rough for exercise, John Slocum stabled his tall horse with the post sutler. Some time toward the middle of January, the Colonel had taken to visiting that stable every other day and finally daily. That was when the stakes in John Slocum's poker game changed.

The games had been nickel, dime, and quarter games: just something to while away the time.

One Saturday night the Colonel strode into the sutler's store and through the beaded curtain that separated the poker room from the rest of the establishment. "I hear you like penny ante poker," he said.

And John Slocum spread his hands flat on the table and smiled. "I play any limit poker you like. I play no limit poker, table stakes."

The canvas bag the Colonel tossed on the table held several thousand dollars. It was a surprising amount of money. It was his inheritance, the Colonel said.

The game was too rich for the ordinary enlisted men to play.

"When your money is gone," the Colonel demanded, "you bet your horse."

"Sure thing," Slocum agreed. "It's just a horse."

There were three players: John Slocum, the post sutler, and post commander.

The Colonel was a terrible card player, but he had awful good cards, and that first night of play he reduced John Slocum's two thousand dollars to a couple hundred.

Next week, they played again, and this time John Slocum won all his money back and dipped into the Colonel's to the tune of a thousand. The sutler pretty well stayed even.

They seesawed back and forth at those Saturday-night games. Slocum never needed to bet his horse, though the cards certainly weren't coming his way. The Colonel was filling open-ended straights and busted flushes and it seemed whenever Slocum had two pair, the Colonel drew three, and found the kicker for his lonely pair.

The second week of February, Saturday night, John Slocum cleaned the Colonel out. Every cent.

The Colonel didn't like that so much, and he was the post commander.

Suddenly John Slocum found that the livery needed the room and would no longer stable his horse. Then he learned that his sleeping quarters was needed for storage. He heard there'd be a little difficulty purchasing hay and grain for his horse.

John Slocum considered shooting the Colonel, but decided against it. When Bill Hickok shot a couple pony soldiers down in Kansas they chased him for six months, and the soldiers were privates. He'd never sleep easy again if he put a bullet in the Colonel.

So he rode south toward the railroad. It was slow, hard going, and only fortunate weather made it possible at all. He was running very low on oats and coffee when he spotted a soddy roof on the open plains. There were better than a hundred head of cattle behind the soddy, but he didn't give them a second thought.

When he found out who was living in that soddy, he should have thought about the cattle, but it honestly never crossed his mind. Billy and Pat had been a couple of Quantrill's wildest raiders. Which, since these raiders included men like Jesse and Frank, and Cole and Jim Younger, was saying quite a lot. Most of Quantrill's men who'd survived the war had turned outlaw. It never crossed Slocum's mind that Billy and Pat might have swung a wide loop too.

Sometimes a man can be mighty stupid and mighty lucky, like the colonel had been. Like, until that soddy, John Slocum had been. He and Billy and Pat had ridden together, but so had a hundred others, and they'd never got to be close during the War. Now, in this remote winter-bound soddy, they became the best of friends. They broke out the whiskey and told lies until night was fading into morning. Each discovered virtues in the other they had never quite appreciated before. They laughed at jokes everyone knew by heart and recalled all their long-dead acquaintances. They never talked about the present, not a word.

The next afternoon, Mountain Jack rode toward the soddy with a big party of men.

"Looks like a posse to me," Slocum observed, peering out the window.

"Likely is." Pat laughed. He was stuffing rounds into his rifle. Billy was buckling his gunbelt.

Not until then did John Slocum recall the fine cattle he'd seen on his ride in. Very stupid.

"Oh, shit," he said.

"Don't you worry none," Pat said. "We'll take care of it."

"They ain't your cattle, are they?"

"They're our cattle if we kill all the men in that posse," Pat said.

John Slocum just looked at him. "This ain't my affair, Pat," he said.

Pat levered one in the chamber. "Never thought it was," he said. "Maybe you better just ride on out of here."

Good advice. John Slocum was trying to follow it when the bullet smacked him in the chest and nearly cured all his ignorance on the spot—the only way, finally, that it can be cured.

He opened his eyes again and watched the woman-child bustling around the cabin. "You a Crow?" he asked in that tongue.

"Half Snake," she answered cheerfully. "My father was white."

John Slocum's black hair doubtless came from Cherokees who intermarried back before Andy Jackson's time when the eastern tribes and the whites had equal strength and honored treaties. Plenty of Cherokees married whites in the Georgia hills in those days. But that black hair was the only sign of Indian blood John Slocum still carried, though it was evidence enough to get him admitted to most tribal councils.

His own folks claimed to be white through and through

but, like the girl, John Slocum was part breed, generations back.

Half-breeds took the lowest jobs, lay in the poorest cribs, did the roughest kind of work. The railroad wasn't awful particular who they hired but the Army wanted white men and only hired a few full-bloods for scouts.

She had a hard row to hoe. He tried to guess the girl's age. A child yet, just on the verge of being a woman. Black hair, startlingly blue eyes. In another year or so, she'd be a real man-killer.

A heavy thump on the door and a snowy boy came in bringing the cold right in with him. He was almost too weary to stand and the cold pinched his features and made him seem older. He would have fallen without the one hand set against the wall. When he unwrapped his muffler, John Slocum could see damage. Some of the skin on his forehead and neck was dead white: frostbite, for certain. His hands were bloody and several nails were broken so deep they had bled. "I got it," he said, and the words stumbled over his tongue. "All but the head. I couldn't move the head, so I piled snow over it. You can't see it. The tracks are almost filled where I dragged the sled." If his sister hadn't been there to support him, the boy would surely have fallen.

She stripped him raw where he sat, pulling every bit of wet, frozen cloth off his body. Neither seemed embarrassed at the boy's nakedness. His eyes were glazed and he breathed through his open mouth, tiny puffs of breath, as she rubbed him down with a flannel cloth dipped in hot water.

She worked silently, like she'd performed this job many times before. Slocum thought it likely that she had.

"They'll never find it now," the boy said. "The ass half's in one gully and the front half's in another and the legs are gone, too." His bleary eyes didn't register any particular surprise at Slocum's wakefulness. "How'd you come to have so much gold in your saddlebags?" he asked. A boy's normal curiosity flared in his dark eyes.

"Won it from a man who wanted my horse."

The boy laughed and gagged. "Well, he can have him now," he said.

The boy looked awful, but he was young, and once the girl got some horse broth in him he started to perk right up. He scratched the places where his skin had frozen and set the flannel cloth in his lap to cover his groin.

The weariness stayed in the slow cadence of his speech and the way he slurred the endings of his words. "Who you runnin' from, mister?" he asked.

"Some fellows who don't claim to be friends of mine," Slocum replied. Just because he was helpless, flat on his back, didn't mean he was going to answer rude questions. He'd traveled too many hard trails to put up with that.

"My brother has been to town," the girl explained. "Men there hunt a cattle rustler named Slocum. You have a watch engraved to Captain Slocum."

"And they're sons of bitches," the boy said in his monotonous tone. "Little Will, he's the worst of the lot."

"Dark-casted man? About my age—dapper dresser?" Slocum described the man who'd first shot him.

"Yes," the boy said. "He is younger than you. You are old."

Remembering how he must look, John Slocum tried on a smile. "In Point of Rocks I mistook their intentions. I thought I could scare them off. I should have nailed them all."

The girl had a funny expression on her pensive face. She opened her hand and a chunk of gray-black metal lay there. "This is the bullet," she said.

"You got it out?"

"Me and Lacey."

Slocum blinked. He said, "I am in your debt."

"Four thousand dollars' worth?" Lacey asked.

Shocked, his sister put her hand up like she'd call back the words. "Lacey! That's terrible."

The boy looked down at his shoes. "If my money's all you want," Slocum said, "You know where it is."

The boy kept his eyes lowered but said, "I'm sorry. My head is spinning and my tongue flaps loose. We do not wish your money. I was afraid of that man, Little Will. I thought he was a cruel man and so I did not tell them of you. Jessica said we should keep our silence until we learned who you were. If they find you here, they will not be gentle with us. What kind of man are you?"

Now that was a hell of a question to ask a wounded man. Slocum closed his eyes. What did they want? What would satisfy them?

He spoke of the home place: Slocum's Stand, it had been called: prime Georgia mountain land with a big house and a springhouse and the forge and the icehouse where they packed the ice in sawdust after they cut it off Little Chilly Draft. His homeplace. He wondered if he'd ever know another place he could call home.

The War had swept him up. Him and his brother Robert too, ignorant kids full of fire. They learned a few things, some they might have been better off not knowing, before Robert was killed at a little crossroads called Gettysburg while John Slocum's sharpshooters tried to clear a way for them.

He told them about Robert. He spoke of how it was riding with Quantrill in the closing days of the War. He told them of Frank James's laugh and little Jesse James, who used to dress up like a woman to scout Union posts.

He described what Lawrence, Kansas looked like after they sacked it; obeying Bloody Bill Anderson's fearsome command that they should kill every man-thing in Lawrence. The wailing women, the smoke that hung low on the streets and choked you like no smoke before or since. He told them about what Bloody Bill's head looked like after Yankee troopers had it mounted on the iron fence spike.

"I went back home after the War," he said. "There was nothing for me there."

He'd ridden back to Slocum's Stand: a tall, dusty rider

riding one weary footsore horse and leading another one. Those horses and his guns were all he'd taken out of four years of war. Oh, he'd taken his life, too, but after that much bitter warfare, his own life didn't seem so very valuable to him any more. He had loosened most of his holds on this world.

His mama and daddy had succumbed to a wasting disease while he was away. Now he stood above their graves, scarcely settled into the ground in the old family graveyard on the slope above the wide place where Little Chilly Draft was prettiest in the spring. The headstones were gray granite marked with only their initials and dates. Cheap gravestones and an early passing—that's what the War had meant to them.

John Slocum worked. He worked to plow his oat and corn ground. He worked to tear up ruined rail fences and cannabalized rails until he had enough for two safe pastures. He rebuilt the bear-proof hog barn. His horses plowed, hauled, carried, and pulled. Fine cavalry animals used that way.

One fine day a pleasant-faced man came riding down to the barn. Him and his hardcase sidekick. The man said he was interested in owning Slocum's Stand. Seems he thought it'd make good high summer pasture for his horses which he'd raced up north and meant to race this year in Louisville and Nashville. The man was a Yank, a judge, part of the reconstruction administration. The hardcase was his assistant.

Slocum said no. "I got my work now, if you don't mind."

Pleasant-faced judge said how Slocum's daddy had never paid a cent of taxes on the home place all through the War and he had records to prove it. Pleasant-faced judge offered John Slocum two hundred dollars for a quit claim on five hundred acres of fairly good improved land, house, and outbuildings.

The house had been built by John Slocum's great-great-grandaddy. Some of the logs in the loft still had loopholes from fighting the Indians.

"Two hundred dollars ain't much of a price," Slocum said mildly.

"Better'n nothin'," the judge replied. "See you next Wednesday. That'll give you time to pack."

But when the two Yanks rode back into the farmyard on the Wednesday, the man they met wasn't the same as the lanky farmer they'd spoken with before.

The man they met was six foot one inch of pure meanness. Mocking green eyes and a mocking kind of stance and a brace of Colt Navy revolvers, model 1860, that weren't mocking at all.

The hardcase made a try. That's what he was paid for. Though the judge was paid for slipping past the law, stealing with his broad-nibbed pen, the judge made a try, too.

John Slocum killed them both, just as quick as he killed whatever future he might have had in that part of the country.

"It didn't work out at home," John Slocum told the two breed kids. "Afterwards, I came West. Handled some horses and cows."

He'd brought two good herds out of Texas. Brush-popping wild cows out of the chaparral through Spanish daggers that'd cut a man's arms and legs to pieces. Pushing them cross-country to the railroad. Indians and rustlers were the least of their hazards. Weather killed. Sometimes trouble among the crew had to be handled by the rough and ready. John Slocum had buried a few men in his day. Slocum kept a single double eagle so nobody else would have to tip the undertaker when his own time came. He'd loved a few women and fought beside a few men.

"I sold some remounts up in Fort Bozeman and was on my way to the railroad when I ran up against the gent who shot me."

He spoke about how angry he was when Pat and Dilly brought him into a fight that was none of his concern. He explained the feeling of shock when the bullet slugged him senseless: how, unconsciously, he'd wrapped his hands in the horse's mane and leaned forward over his neck. "There's some fellows you can walk away from and some you can't," he said. "Some fellows get real ferocious when you show them your back, and it's worth a man's life to distinguish that kind. Me and Pat and Billy could have sent them boys packing in the first place and wouldn't have heard no more, but I didn't want to fight over another man's cows. That was my mistake, I reckon. You found my gold, so I expect you prowled my saddlebags. You find anything like a pistol in there?"

The boy nodded.

"You bring it over here and set it beside me. Them fellows come around here, we'll put a stop to them."

Eagerly, the boy went for the gun. The girl stepped beside the cot where she'd propped her patient. She offered her thumb. "Take it," she said. "Hang on to my thumb."

John Slocum made a fist around her child's thumb and though he squeezed as hard as he could, she lifted it right out of his fist. He had no strength.

The boy unwrapped the Colt Navy. He hesitated and rewrapped it again.

The girl smiled. "I think you'll be our guest for a few more days. I think it'll be a while before you can protect us."

John Slocum scowled.

"Do you want more broth? I believe I'll have some now, and then we can all go to sleep. Lacey, will the sled burn?" she asked.

"It was live pine," Lacey replied. "It'll burn, but won't throw much heat."

"Tomorrow morning you must saw it up. Captain Slocum, would you like more broth?"

The whore, Sallie Arthur, was a realist. A romantic realist.

She'd always fallen for hardcases, ne'er-do-wells, and men who laughed easily and abandoned her just as easily. She had seen a few men in her day.

"Mister Little Will Japhe," she said, "if you don't mind, I'll not take a drink with you tonight. I am not in a drinking mood."

The saloon bar at Paxton's was filled with discouraged searchers. Some hadn't bothered to change their sodden clothes before they came here. These worthies were backed up to the pot-bellied stove in a semicircle, bitching about weary muscles and bruises. One man had frostbitten fingers. The sawdust was slick with their dripping and the air was full of steam. The wet sat on Vinegar Varese's forehead as he worked the bar and wetness had taken all the shape out of William Paxton's white shirt.

Little Will had taken a place at the poker table where he burned the low-stakes nickel-and-dime games by betting too much every time he had a sure winner.

The searchers had reached Miner's Delight by noon and had spent no more than half an hour at that outpost. The men at Miner's Delight stopped work to visit with the men from their sister camp. "What's the news?" they wanted to know. There were drinks and coffee offered and a dry place out of the snow, but the searchers had no time to exchange more than unsatisfactorily brief information before they had to turn around if they were to make it back to South Pass before dark.

Somebody at Miner's Delight said the western railroad was still making progress east, though the eastern railroad had stopped all operations for the winter.

That scrap of news brought to South Pass created disputes about the Chinese laborers' role in the continued progress of the western. Some were quick to admire the Chinese but most thought the Irish made better railroad men, and some said Chinamen were a great threat to the working man.

The searchers were pretty damn surly. It hadn't been a

very good day. They tried to keep their surliness in check. That crazy bastard Will Japhe was black with anger and anger leaked out from every polite phrase and the way he tossed his gold piece into the pot to capture a dollar and ten cents in two-bit pieces, dimes, and nickels.

Vinegar Varese kept Little Will's glass filled, coming our from behind the bar to do it, though he'd never been known to perform that service for any other man.

Vinegar Varese had been bought. When Little Will left South Pass, the fire-scarred giant was to accompany him. Little Will thought he would be a smash hit in London. He particularly looked forward to bringing his new manservant to his club.

Vinegar Varese had taken Little Will up on his offer straightaway. William Paxton was secretly relieved.

"Do serve from the left, man. And stand back when you're finished, or change your brand of cologne."

Vinegar said, "Yes, sir," which was another first.

Nobody joked. Not with Vinegar's temper and that ash cudgel under the bar.

Coats steamed in the heat. Men conversed in low tones. After one day, the searchers had given up. It was barely possible the fugitive had crossed South Pass and got down to lower country before the snow caught him. Just the other side of South Pass, the Oregon Trail split, one half going through Utah, the other, Lander's cutoff, going north to avoid Mormon country. Lander's cutoff was surveyed when the army got all worked up about Mormon attacks on their surveyors.

Maybe John Slocum had been killed by the Indians. Maybe he'd stumbled into a Crow hunting party. Maybe he was bowstrings by now.

But probably he'd frozen and his horse had yarded up and would starve, and come spring they'd find the little circle of trees with the bark chewed off and the pile of horse bones. They'd find Slocum bleached and scattered with his horse.

Just another dead rustler. The searchers wondered if his bones would still be worth one thousand dollars. It didn't seem likely.

What had begun as a day's break from routine had turned sour. More than one of the searchers wished Lord Japhe and his son hadn't ever showed their aristocratic faces in the town of South Pass.

Little Will got to his feet when Sallie Arthur walked into the room. "Evening," he said. "I know we haven't been formally introduced, but I'd like to buy you a dram."

That was when she gave her answer. "I'd rather not get you thinking wrong about what that'd buy you," she added.

Little Will flushed. "I believe, madam," he said stonily, "you are for sale."

She cocked her hip saucily. "Never for sale. Sometimes for rent. And, sir, I am extremely particular about my tenants. They may not all be nobility, but their hands are clean."

She swept up to the bar and the listeners roared with laughter that had been repressed too long. Men said Sallie was a real sport and she basked in the glow. Old friends bought her drinks. Vinegar wore an anxious look in his eyes and the lower corner of his eyelid trembled. He would have done Sallie Arthur some hurt, admirers or no admirers, if the Englishman had wished it, but Little Will turned on his heel and marched from the room. The men laughed harder. Vinegar Varese glared, but he went on serving drinks, and even William Paxton wore a grin.

7

Every day, any time after noon, the still air shivered to the distant boom of avalanches. The new snow had no more settled than it started to melt. Sunny days one after another.

It was hard on men's nerves. The early thaw had brought men out of their hibernation too soon and too soon set them slumbering again. Cautious men mended their snowshoes. Even the greatest optimists didn't start digging country rock for the sluices.

When the third day went by without the half-breeds showing up for work, William Paxton hired a drunk to perform the swamper's tasks. He paid him a little better than he had paid the boy, though the work he did was lower quality than the boy had done and every time Paxton wanted the spittoons emptied he had to order the job done. Grudgingly, the drunk accommodated him muttering all the while, "This ain't no fit work for a white man, no, sirree."

One morning Mountain Jack and Sallie saw a flight of geese heading north. "Them birds are a trifle premature," Jack opined.

"By God," she said in a soft whisper, "it's spring."

"It's March," he said. "Can't be spring. Now you come

117

back to this bed here. I got a little present for you."

Sallie turned away from the window and grinned. "What's so little about that?" she asked. But she half turned her face to the window and said, "Jack, I'm worried about those damn kids. Maybe they've got themselves sick or something. You want to go out there this afternoon?"

"I ain't got no plans to do anything this afternoon," he said. "I don't know how you're gonna get me out of bed."

Lord Japhe had taken to reading the Bible every morning downstairs in Paxton's. Never in the saloon, where he spent his long, quiet afternoons; he did his Bible reading in the lobby.

William Paxton, that enthusiast, made a point of entering the lobby after he knew Lord Japhe had been in there for a full sixty minutes. Paxton didn't think anyone could read the Bible for longer than that. He didn't think anyone had it in him. He would stride into the modest lobby that served his Inn and step behind the desk with a cheery "Good morning."

Lord Japhe would close his Bible. Sometimes he'd add a sigh so faint Paxton could scarcely hear it.

Paxton would run his finger down the register which, because of the snow, showed the same entries each day as it had the day before—and, for that matter, the same entries it had shown the previous week.

"Jack Cunningham, Poison Springs, Wyoming Territory," Paxton read aloud. "If I was the first one to settle that part of the country, I wouldn't want to name it Poison Springs, no sirree. How you gonna attract development capital to any place named Poison Springs? I intend to print up a description of South Pass in that new brochure the Union Pacific is gonna put out. Their Cheyenne agent asked me last fall to ready my contribution for a time it might be needed." He puffed himself up. "Just between you and me, Lord Japhe, South Pass isn't quite paradise on earth. Sensitive souls might describe it as downright homely. Like a miner said, 'It's ugly but it's got pretty quartz.' Do you think I'll remark about its physical beauty for lack of same in my contribution? No, sir. Let sleeping dogs lie, that's what I say."

His lordship said, "Paxton, you aren't, by any chance, a religious man?" He held up the heavy black book.

Paxton blew out his chest. "Lord Japhe," he said, "I am a free thinker. I believe in the evidence, sir. Just live it like you can and every man has his own authority. No popery." Paxton had no particular feelings about Catholics one way or another but he didn't like the Irish and had heard the term "papists" applied to them.

Lord Japhe seized his opportunity. "I have Catholic antecedents, sir," he said with a snap in his voice that shut Paxton's mouth except for a stammered apology.

Neck burning, the younger man examined his register for thirty seconds, the lines swimming in his sight. His scalp itched. He'd just meant to be friendly and accommodating, and here this Englishman was treating him rough. He glanced up, hoping to catch his lordship's eye, but the man was already at it again, reading his Bible, legs crossed, in a casual attitude. Maybe his lordship thought "Our Lord" was just a fellow nobleman.

With a sneer he was afraid to utter, William Paxton fled the lobby on new shoes which squeaked from time to time.

Lord Japhe read his Bible, desolate in his soul. He read Ecclesiastes, because the counsel of that embittered preacher was balm to him.

His son played penny-ante poker with Vinegar Varese. Little Will was much the superior player and a skilled cheat as well. He won with great regularity, pots of ten or twenty cents, sometimes half a dollar. He financed the ugly man, keeping track in his pocket address book. Vinegar Varese already owed Little Will three months' wages. His employer already owned every cent the fire-scarred man had had in his pockets.

As they played, Little Will talked. Vinegar Varese was so ugly and so scarred that it was easy to forget he was human at all. It was easy to treat the man as if he belonged to some other species—an exceptionally intelligent ape, say. At first, when Little Will got to talking, Vinegar Varese would grunt or say "That so?" or "Hell, I never thought of it that way before," as his modest contribution to discourse. But each time he spoke, Little Will clamped his lips tight. One "That so?" and the game would go silent for half an hour or so until Little Will, lulled by the silence, once more became indiscreet.

Since Vinegar Varese liked to hear what the young nobleman was saying, he learned to keep silent—to play the subhuman or the mute.

Little Will talked to Vinegar Varese the same way he'd talked to his batman in the British Army, another subhuman, a Gurkha who pretended not to speak a word of English. Coporal Timura had been privileged to see all the twists and windings of the master's soul. One day, in a fit of temper, the Corporal threw it up to Lieutenant Japhe and Little Will had killed the man quick.

Lord Japhe had hushed up the affair and, soon afterwards, Little Will had found himself traveling to America with his dull father.

Little Will couldn't confide the secrets of his life to his father because his father was, after all, human. But he missed his batman, his subhuman. Thus, Vinegar Varese was a find, and Little Will made up for lost time, hour after hour at the poker table stripping Vinegar's small salary away, mechanically and gracefully, as he told all once again.

His mother and father had been a love match, more intertwined with each other than with their son, who'd been raised by nannies, governesses, and tutors. He'd seduced his first servant, a kitchen wench, when he was just a stripling of fourteen. When the girl's father complained, the man came to him rather than Lord Japhe, and it was the boy himself who bought the man off. From then on, the boy had taken one after another of the servant maids and the village girls, finally setting himself the difficult—some might say impossible—task of seducing every girl of his age in the neighborhood.

Vinegar Varese was fascinated. Little Will was a good story teller, fluid of countenance and acting out all the parts. He told of virgins and whores, described their breasts and the way their skin felt under his hand—"So smooth, so smooth . . ."

And Vinegar Varese would nod his head eagerly. Nods were permitted. Even a dog can nod.

Little Will expressed his philosophy of life. "There are only two sorts. Our sort, and the other sort. And," he laughed, "There aren't so many of our sort any more."

Vinegar Varese stretched his face in a parody of a smile. Though he wasn't really "our sort," he hoped to be included in that band through oversight. Maybe if he stood close enough to Little Will, he'd be taken for "our sort" by mistake.

Little Will told of the Sepoy Mutiny and how they'd punished the mutineers. "We just strapped them across the muzzles of the cannon, don't you see. Touched them off in a glorious salute, a hundred guns at a time. You'd have thought it would have been grisly, the cannon ball passing through the wogs' parts, but it wasn't. It just vaporized all the intestines and those sorts of things so there weren't any repulsive parts dangling around or spattering the gunners' uniforms. But if the wind was coming from the east, it'd pick up their blood vapor, and in the instant after the guns fired, before the noise had quite died away, we'd be covered in a mist of blood. You could feel it on your face like rain. And, of course, smell it, too. Everybody in dress regimental uniform at rigid attention. The coolies unstrapped the cadaver from the muzzle of the gun and the private soldiers brought up another poor blighter. I think I will never forget that blood mist. Tiny little specks. The Sergeant Major's face and handlebar moustache turned red, shot after shot. We cannoned a thousand men in one day. I am a lucky man to have been part of that."

Little Will talked of blood and rape. Unlike his batman, Corporal Timura, who had been known before his untimely demise as a man of sense, Vinegar Varese was excitable. He was thrilled by Little Will's accounts and wished he had led the nobleman's life. Sensing the brute's admiration, Little Will told Vinegar Varese a few especially dark tales. There was that dusky young girl in the gatekeeper's lodge that night and her father off somewhere and the two of them quite alone. Little Will could have been hanged if that story ever got out. And there was the time in Punjab, with the woman hostage and her daughter. It was true enough that her husband had gone over to the other side and the officials had termed it joint suicide, but if there'd been any kind of investigation at all, Little Will would have swung.

The two bad men made themselves steadily worse. Other men who came into Paxton's to nurse a short whiskey ignored the two of them muttering in the corner. The odor coming out of that particular corner was pretty strong, and wise men shunned it.

The icicles were melting. Once again snow was sliding off the steep roofs into the street. Bare spots were forming in the street. The stink of spring mud was in the air. Life was going to come back again this year. Johnson, of Johnson's Livery, asked Sallie Arthur for a quick one before noon. Johnson had scrubbed himself down and stood before her with his hair combed straight back and glistening with pomade.

"I'd like to, Johnson," Sallie said, "but I'm kind of tangled up with the one fellow now, Mountain Jack. Least he's staying in my room just like he was payin' some of the rent, which he ain't. I don't believe I could ask him to get out of the room long enough for you and me to make love."

Sensibly, Johnson suggested his livery.

"Hay is kind of scratchy," Sallie observed judiciously. "Naw, I think me and Jack, we got something between us. It wouldn't be right," she concluded. "If you want to, though, you can take a hike this afternoon. I'm goin' out to see how Lacey and Jessica are doin' at that dugout of theirs. There's enough melt by now I can make it. Mountain Jack won't go with me and I'd like a little company."

But Johnson, who'd scrubbed himself with some thoroughness, hoping to see Sallie all pink, nude, and welcoming, was too disappointed to settle for a hike through the woods. He made excuses.

Sallie implored Mountain Jack a second time but he said that it was fool's work stumbling through the snow. If she had a mind to, she could do it, but he'd stay right here, thanks.

Sallie packed a basket of food. She had the cook make up a hamper of boiled ham, bread, some elk and pork sausage, and two bottles of chokecherry preserves. She put on long johns and men's canvas pants and borrowed a pair of hip boots.

She wore one flannel shirt over another and had a knitted cap for her ears. With the addition of a stout stick, again borrowed, she was ready.

Climbing the first ridge, still within sight of town, she began to hurt. The snow made movement terribly awkward. It was sticky with the melt, the top inches the soggiest, and her boots slogged against the constant pull.

As she struggled through the stubborn snow, she began to picture how it must have been for Lacey and Jessica, making this trip every day despite the changeable weather. She began to wonder about the dugout and what it must look like. She remembered how infrequent the children's absences had been, and her concern deepened into genuine worry.

On top she took a breather. Up here she could see for

miles across the snow-covered hummocks until the foothills blended with the base of the mountains. One mountain had a plume of snow blowing at the very peak.

The snow had drifted on the ridgetop, but by watching pretty close, Sallie was able to get along the spine of the ridge without getting into snow deeper than a couple of inches. She put off the descent into the first gully but finally had no choice, and she strode onto the uncertain, steep slope. It was just as sticky here as on the back slope and she couldn't hardly pick up enough momentum for a real fall.

It was the color that caught her eye. The color was partway up the opposite slope. She was worried about the gully now. Under the snow was some fairly nasty footing and so she was probing with her staff and the flash of color was just a bird. That was all her distracted eye told her.

She probed across the gully bottom, identifying where the slope resumed. She made her way across without mishap.

A red or purple something. What bird was red or purple? There were a few birds with lavender in them. Could it be a dead teal lying in the snow, the sun making the feathers look redder than they were?

It was meat. Frozen meat. A shadow passed over her, a black shadow on the snow. One vulture had seen it, too. Just one, but soon it would be joined by others of its kind. Sallie wondered what animal lay dead under the snow. Some woods buffalo, torn apart by wolves? A flayed rabbit, eviscerated by a fox? The piece above the snow was so small, no larger than she could cover with one hand, just a chunk of meat glistening in the spring sun. It was very slightly puckered and, up close, much darker than it had seemed from afar. Pure curiosity moved her up that slope to see what kind of animal had ended its life here. Anything that made this climb less painful was worth noting.

She couldn't tell at first. She brushed snow back and scooped it away. She came to the fetlocks, sawed off at the cannon bone, and a horrible sinking feeling rose in her throat. It was part of a dead horse. A cut-up dead horse. How and why?

Some strange Indian ritual? Some madman in the woods? Sallie Arthur had her double derringer in her muff, but she hadn't checked its loads in months.

It was disconcerting to stumble across the forequarters of a dead horse, half buried in the snow. The carcass gave Sallie little information. The chest and forelegs of a dead horse. Somebody had sawed off the feet. That was all.

Despite the bad feeling in her stomach, she went on. She feared for the children. Their absence and this horse added up to bad trouble. If it had been summer, and an easy walk back to town, she might have returned for Mountain Jack, but she'd come too far to turn around now.

As she panted onto the next ridge and easier walking, fears raced through her heart and chilled her despite the sun burning overhead and the glistening of the snow. Her eyes hurt.

In the next gully she found more of the horse. The snow had melted away from the animal's tail and it bristled against the snow like a black otter's pelt. Just the root of the tail and the beginning of the dead horse's plume shone in the snow.

She made slow time through the woods because the sun hadn't penetrated so far here, but she came on as quick as she could, pressing her wicker basket to her waist, one hand wrapped around the butt of her derringer.

The smoke rising steadily from the chimney didn't reassure her. Indian war parties liked a fire too—plenty paths through the snow—woodhauling paths, littered with bark and needle debris.

The trails collected at the front door of the cabin where

there was a great pile of fir branches too small to bother with. On the other side of the door a horse's head leered at her. Its eyes were glazed. The froth frozen at its nose and mouth was bloody and black. The ears stood straight up like they had a will of their own.

The head was like a heathen idol, a guardian or, perhaps, a sacrifice.

Sallie Arthur went weak in the knees. She simply stood in the snow looking at the horse's head. Finally, it made her mad. Angrily, she pulled her pathetic derringer from her fur muff and marched right up to the cabin door, ready to avenge the children if that was what was called for.

Behind her, in the forest, a bird sang. Somewhere, deeper, a woodpecker rapped away at frozen bark, like a distant string of firecrackers.

The latchstring was out and she stomped right on inside before she had time to think and maybe talk herself out of it.

"Sallie!" The girl looked up from her tattered book, amazed.

Lacey had one boot covered thick with bear grease. He placed the finished boot on a piece of bark at his feet. Bear grease was awfully messy until it set up.

A strange man was propped up in the bed. His black hair had more life than the paleness of his sick white face. "Who the hell are you?" Sallie demanded, ignoring the fact that this wasn't her house, that she had just crashed in; ignoring everything in her relief at finding the children alive.

"Might ask you the same." The man tried a faint smile which just about matched his faint voice. His upper torso was rudely bandaged with what looked to be cut-up long johns.

Sallie lifted her derringer to arm's length and pointed its muzzle right at the junction of the man's head and throat. The muzzle didn't tremble a bit. "I'm Sallie Arthur, formerly of Arkansas and the Nations. Now, who might you be?"

"John Slocum."

The girl chimed in, "Captain Slocum—that's what we call him."

Sallie lowered her derringer. "Oh, Lord save us!" she said.

The fire roared but Sallie didn't feel the warmth. Some kind of meat broth was cooking on the stove. The smell of it made her want to throw up. Except for the invalid's bed, there wasn't a stick of furniture left in the room. The kids' bed was a pallet on the floor. Sallie found her chased silver flask and took a quick hit on it. It burned going down but it didn't clear her head. "When you gonna go?" she asked.

"Soon as I'm able," he replied cheerfully. His voice was weak as a whisper. "Meantime, I been teaching this girl from *Macbeth*. She said you was teaching her the poems."

"Sonnets," she corrected mechanically.

"Yeah. Those. They're awful pretty but I didn't want to be trespassin' on your claim. Me and Jess are studying *Macbeth*."

"Jessica." Again the mechanical correction. She rediscovered her old schoolmarm tone of voice, the one she'd forgotten these many years.

"Yes, ma'am." The sick man grinned at her.

It wouldn't do him any good. This was awful damn serious, and that revolver at his elbow didn't make it less so. "There's one thousand dollars out on you," she said.

He shrugged. The tiniest move of his head constituted the entire shrug. "I suppose that's quite a lot of money," he said with an air of indifference.

"You bet it is," she said. "It's more than a year's wages!"

Again that nearly invisible shrug.

"You know what they'll do to these kids if they find you here?" She grabbed Jessica around the shoulders and held her like an exhibit. "Take a look at this girl's face. Tell me what you see there. She's a half-breed, damn it. Her and Lacey, too. And their mother, their mother was ... well, she wasn't any better than she should have been. Mister, these kids live on the edge every day of their lives, and you have probably pushed them over."

Jessica said, "I'm not afraid to die."

"Me neither," Lacey said.

Just a split second later, in a voice lighter and more childish than Lacey's, John Slocum chimed in, "Me neither."

Sallie Arthur didn't find the joke so amusing as the children, who giggled and looked at each other and giggled some more.

Sallie took another drink. A stiff one. "I suppose that's his horse out there in the snow."

Lacey's face fell. "I carried it so far away. How could you have found it.?"

"Snow melts, sonny. That's one of the things snow's good at."

The boy looked abashed.

His sister said, "Captain Slocum isn't a cattle rustler. He was just riding through."

"Sure, Jessica. I'm sure he isn't a cattle rustler. He has the look of the innocent pilgrim. That Colt beside his hand—why, his sainted mother probably gave him that to keep him safe and bring him home. Oh, Jessica, you're such a child."

The boy pointed at Slocum's saddlebags. "He's got plenty of gold. Nearly four thousand dollars' worth. We counted it."

"He probably just found it lying on the trail. Ain't that right, mister?" Sallie pushed herself at him, face out like an icebreaker.

"Anything you say." He smiled.

The impact of his green eyes stopped her dead in her tracks. He was awful weak, but his eyes glowed with laughter.

"Damn you," she spat. "You think this is funny."

"No, ma'am," he corrected her gently. "I think *you're*

funny." He chanced a small smile. "These two kids saved my bacon, and I'm real grateful to them. I just don't see where you come into this at all."

Sallie drew up to her full height and her eyes flashed a warning. "Come along, Jessica, Lacey. We're getting out of here."

The wounded man made no objection, but Jessica and Lacey made no move to go, not even after Sallie explained that if they were found with the fugitive, likely they'd be hurt bad or worse. Once more, Jessica repeated her litany, "I am not afraid to die."

Lacey agreed.

"Me neither," the man said with a laugh and, despite herself, the corners of Sallie's mouth trembled and she snorted so she wouldn't chuckle.

"Maybe she's right, Jess," Slocum said. "Maybe you should make tracks for town. I can probably keep the fire going." He made a giant effort to sit up and actually got his feet on the floor. The sweat popped out on his forehead. Seated, he swayed, but his smile was steady. "I don't want you two to be in danger on account of me. I was hopin' to get a mite stronger before I met up with that posse, but I expect I can sting 'em some as it is. You go on now. Follow your dear auntie there."

"I ain't their aunt," Sallie snapped.

"Go with grannie, then," Slocum said. "I don't care." The sweat was dripping off his chin and his arms were trembling.

"And I ain't no grandmother either!" This time Sallie howled. She couldn't hit a man hurt this bad, so she had to laugh at him. All her tension and anger dissolved in that laughter. "Oh my," she said, "don't you make me laugh so hard or I'll pee myself."

That brought the kids into the joke and even brought a smile to Slocum's sweaty face. "I ain't no cattle rustler," he said. "They had no call to hunt me."

"That Little Will is a mean bastard. And he's got Vinegar Varese with him now. It's like they was married," Sallie said.

"Vinegar Varese? Big man? Burnt face?"

"That's him."

The wounded man nodded. "I heard something about him. He killed a man in Abilene. Beat his head in with a stick." The knuckles of his hands were white. "The only one in that bunch worth a damn is Mountain Jack. Jack's a man."

Since Sallie had had occasion to verify this view, she smiled and said, "Lie back down now. I'll think of something."

"Maybe I can rebury the horse," Lacey piped up. "Maybe I can move it."

Sallie said, "The buzzards were starting to circle. I reckon they ain't had so big a feast since the fall."

The man sat still, the pain rolling across his eyes in waves. His knuckles were locked to the side rail of the cot.

"Say, mister," Sallie said, "why don't you lie back? We'll take care of things. I believe you. Damn stubborn kids. I can't do anything with them anyway. Besides," she added, "I always did admire a man who read Shakespeare."

Though the kids had just finished their noon meal, Sallie insisted they have some of the food she'd brought in the wicker basket.

When she urged John Slocum to sit back down, he refused. "It's time I got my strength. Man ain't worth much in rough country without his strength."

She couldn't persuade him to rest. She couldn't persuade the children to leave. She couldn't persuade a sick man to lie down. A powerless, confused woman stepped outside to do her thinking. "Nice horsey," she said, and shuddered.

She couldn't tell Mountain Jack because Jack would be honor bound to tell Lord Japhe, and they'd string their wounded quarry to the nearest tree. She thought for a long while and came up empty. No plan appealed to her more than any other. When she went back inside, she said, "Kids, you got yourself in the soup this time."

Jessica had an idea. "Sallie, we'll go to your rooms. We'll hide the Captain there until he's well. If they search here, we will be gone."

"Three days," the wounded man croaked. "Maybe two. Two days and I can fight again." He got to his feet, swayed, but he stood there. "I reckon I can make it a few miles," he said.

"How you gonna get him through the lobby of the hotel?" Sallie asked.

Sure enough, Jessica had a plan for that too.

The two women went on ahead together. John Slocum and the boy were to come in later.

"Remember," Jessica said, "nobody will be watching when the dusk settles below the first ridge. That's when they'll all be looking at me."

And so it was that Sallie Arthur and the half-breed girl entered the lobby of Paxton's Inn at three o'clock that day. They were both wet from the snow, but most folks were wet and nobody commented on it. Lord Japhe was reading his Bible. He didn't even look up. Jessica waited outside while Sallie Arthur burst into her own room, fluffed up like an outraged hen. Hands on hips, she surveyed her home. The bed was unmade. The room stank of havana cigars. She stooped over and picked up an offending object. "Why don't you pick up your filthy socks, you bum?"

Mountain Jack, barefoot, in his long johns, was stretched out in one of her chairs with his feet across another one. He was caught at a disadvantage.

"Jack," she said firmly, "I don't want you livin' here any more. You can get your own room or move in with your English pals. I want you out of here right now."

"Sweetheart—" he began.

"Don't sweetheart me, you filthy, inconsiderate bum.

Get your gear and hit the trail!" she stormed.

Jack had his pride. He may have been undressed, but he didn't have to take this sort of abuse. He gathered his pants and socks and dirty shirts and his jacket and his razor strap and razor and shaving mug and soap and comb and laid them across the bed. He wrapped the whole of his belongings together like a peddler's pack and pushed right by her. As he passed, he leaned over so his mouth was right next to hers and said, "I thought we was gonna be snuggled in till warm weather, just like Mama Bear and Papa Bear."

She was merciless. Deep in her heart she loved Mountain Jack, but she couldn't let anything happen to those kids. She kept her back stiff and listened to him marching down the hall until he reached the back room on the ground floor. When he slammed the door, her own door vibrated.

Jessica grinned at her. "You and me," she said. "We will fool them all."

Sallie shook her head, quite worried. "I dunno," she said. "It's a chancey notion."

The girl clapped her hands together. "It will work. It will. Now, let me see some of your fine clothes."

It was four o'clock, later accounts agreed, when Jessica Tripp descended the stairs of Paxton's Inn as a woman. Lord Japhe glanced up and was, for a moment, pulled away from the consolations of religion. She was young and so vivid. She was as vivid as a high mountain wildflower and as delicate. The skirt was a full skirt and her blouse was white lace, hooked at the neck. Her small breasts pressed the fabric only a little. Her black, black hair was plaited in ringlets which fell on all sides on her face, framing its beauty.

She carried a parasol, grand as any grand lady. She looked like a Latin aristocrat with her high, fine features and those stunning light blue eyes. "Lord Japhe?"

He rose to his feet. "Charmed, I'm sure."

"Would you escort me into the saloon?" she asked. "I

believe a lady shouldn't enter such a place unescorted."

"Cartainly, ma'am. At your service." He offered his arm and she took it, light as a spring leaf on his aged, gnarled arm.

Vinegar Varese and Little Will had the table in the corner to themselves. William Paxton was behind the bar. Three miners sat at the bar. Pretty soon they could get back to work. One miner worked on the rough sketch of a sluicebox, making notes for necessary materials.

The English lord came in with a lovely woman on his arm. At first nobody recognized Jessica Tripp. This creature bore no resemblance to the half-breed scullery maid of their acquaintance.

Paxton said, "Well, I'll be damned."

The miner snapped the point of his pencil.

Little Will stopped dealing.

"I'll have a sip of sherry wine," Jessica said softly.

The English lord's nod meant put it on his account. When the wine arrived, she smiled at William Paxton ever so sweetly and he responded, blushed, then smiled again. She was such a picture.

With her glass she marched to the back of the room, into the shadows, where Little Will got to his feet at her approach. He swept into a bow. "Your servant, ma'am," he said.

She ignored him and spoke directly to the dreadful face of Vinegar Varese. "I have saved money, sir," she began. "Money for passage to Omaha, where decent work may be found for a woman who does not wish to go whoring."

Vinegar Varese couldn't think of a single thing to say, though apparently she expected some response.

"I should be glad to arrange passage for such an enchanting creature," Little Will burbled.

"Without whoring," she said, scarcely missing a beat.

Her face positively glowed in the late afternoon light. At the front table, the miners strained to catch every word.

William Paxton had a glass in his right hand and a towel in the other, and both objects were frozen in place as was Paxton's little "Oh!" of astonishment.

"Some time ago you made me an offer," Jessica said to the brute.

Vinegar Varese's heart paused in its career and he swallowed. Could it be that this amazingly beautiful virgin was going to offer herself to him?

"A double eagle," she said. "I believe that was your offer. If I would show myself naked to you."

Dumbly, he nodded his head.

"When the shadow touches the top of the ridge," she said, pointing out the front window, "I will return to this place and I will publicly show myself. For twenty dollars gold."

And she hurled her sherry glass into Vinegar Varese's eyes as seriously as she'd made her announcement, spun on her heel, and was gone before Vinegar had time to wipe his sleeve across his face.

"Damn me," Little Will said. Something close to awe in his voice.

The ridge was perfectly plain across the creek, steeps full of snow filled prospect holes. "The sun'll touch that ridgetop about five," a miner said.

William Paxton said, "That's just when it gets dark."

She did it, too. Full house, five o'clock.

She was very deliberate, loosening each stay, and her face never lost its poise as her fingers worked.

John Slocum and Lacey got down the ridge, across the main street of South Pass, through the lobby, and up the stairs of the town's only hotel.

Not twenty hards away, young Jessica bared herself to sixty men's eyes.

Men walked around, like a gentleman's Sunday stroll, like art lovers first viewing a new nude statue.

There were men in that crowd who would have touched her, just to find out if all that beauty was indeed flesh. But Lord Japhe had loaded a pistol, and he would have used it.

8

Men talked of Jessica's act the next morning almost with reverence.

Quite a few spoke about her eyes, though her eyes were always visible and they might have seen them at any time before she took off all her clothes. Many of the men hadn't seen a naked woman since the fall, some even longer than that. There weren't many women in front of the railroad and their charms came dear—too dear for many a man who watched the Indian girl that night.

Quite a few others had fallen in love. These men had been so taken by the girl's beauty that they wanted to take matters a step or two further. When she came down the stairs the next morning, about eleven o'clock, the lobby was crammed with gifts. The lobby desk was covered and a pile filled the corner directly across from where Lord Japhe had sat all night, his pistol in his lap.

They were the gifts love-struck men give with a few minutes' thought and notice. One man had carefully wrapped his personal shaving mirror in a five-pound ore sack and tied the gray canvas with a scrap of bright red twine. The brass-framed shaving mirror was the prettiest thing he owned.

Two different men had thought to give her copies of the New Testament, for rather different reasons. One meant to offer her salvation; the other had the names of his family inscribed in the flyleaf back to 1680, when they'd landed in Massachusetts. It was his old and contented family he offered her. Another wrapped a bit of lace. The lace had been attached to his mother's bridal veil.

There were four watches and half a dozen rings. One man had given her a small revolver with which she might defend herself. Others gave her knives.

She was quite amazed. She said, "But I do not wish any of these things. I have been paid my twenty dollars."

"You must not reject them, child," said the nobleman, whose own gift was subtler. He'd stayed awake all night long, assuring her a peaceful sleep.

Some men had admired her breasts. They were small and high on her rather flat and bony chest. Her thighs were skinnier than most men preferred, skinny and too muscular. Several thought she looked more like a boy than a girl. They judged this on the basis of her thighs and her butt, which was high and rather pert, too.

Some of the rougher types gazed fixedly on her lightly covered mound of venus. Her pudenda was plump and just beginning to separate where it dipped between her legs. Some men would have paid her another twenty dollars in gold for just opening her legs wide apart so they could see just a little better, but there were others in that room who would have shot them dead for simply making the honest offer.

When she came down the next morning, she didn't wear the same outfit as the night before—Sallie's light green gown and the lace blouse. She wore her rough man's pants and flannel shirt and miner's boots again. She meant to go back out to the cabin for John Slocum's saddlebags—or at least the neat rolls of gold coins.

"I can't take all these," she said. "I have nothing to give in return."

"I see," his lordship said. "There are men in this town who would die for you, child."

She made an irritated face. "All this winter I worked for four bits a day. It's nice to be loved."

"We will be leaving here today," Lord Japhe said. "It will mean an overnight camp at Pacific Springs, but we will be in Point of Rocks by noon tomorrow. Coming here has been a mistake. You and your brother can travel with us."

Last month the prospect of accompanying a large armed party to the railhead would have seemed like a dream come true. But she could not, and said so. She said she would stay here until more of the snow was gone.

Lord Japhe said the trail would be clear most of the way. "Why, we might even get to Point of Rocks before sunset."

Upstairs, the night before, two children and a whore had saved a wounded man's life. Jessica stripped while Lacey brought John Slocum to Sallie Arthur's bed.

They'd peeled him out of his soaked clothes. His flesh was a cold grayish-blue.

While Jessica bared her beauty, Lacey and Sallie rubbed the man's frozen extremities. They wrestled him under the covers and piled all the blankets they had over him, but his face stayed dead pale.

"He ain't generating enough heat for the blankets to do him much good," Sallie had said. "Turn your back, boy. A lady is about to disrobe."

While his sister stripped downstairs and Sallie Arthur peeled off her clothes in her bedroom, Lacey Tripp faced the enameled door of Sallie's room, staring at the hand smudges near the knob. He heard the rustle of silken garments. He listened pretty hard, too. Those garments hitting the floor brought him right back from his own exhaustion.

She slipped under the covers with the frozen man and hugged him to her. "I heard of this being done once," she explained through gritted teeth. "The person who told me never said if it was any fun or not."

The man's skin was cold deep down and his breathing sounded like hell. He panted like an overheated cat. From time to time he would tremble right there in her arms. The wound wasn't so hot—it was dead cold, maybe the coldest part of him.

She'd hold him until she couldn't stand the bone-cold any more and then she'd pull back and rub herself under the covers to keep herself going.

When Jessica came back up the stairs, her brother took her by the waist and hugged her.

"How'd it go?" Sallie asked.

"It didn't bother me," Jessica said. "Once I got to doing it, it wasn't bad at all. I just went somewhere else. So now I'm twenty dollars richer." She shrugged. "His face looks terrible."

"I sure hope he don't die after all this."

It was plain enough what Sallie Arthur was hoping to do. She meant to raise John Slocum's temperature to the point where he might commence to living again, through her own body heat. Two can play that game as well as one.

The two women spent most of the night sandwiching the man between them, shivering, withdrawing, and Lacey sat just outside the door, with his back to it, his father's musket across his lap, waiting for the step that never came.

In the morning things looked brighter. Their patient had a little color back in his flesh and once he rallied long enough to open his eyes. He licked his lips, looked for just a moment like he wanted to speak, and then his eyes clicked shut again.

"He's comin' around," Sallie said wearily.

"How do you know?"

"Are you sure?"

"Oh, he'll cheat the hangman this go-around," Sallie said. "If I stay under these covers with him one more minute, I'm gonna be in a situation that'd surprise him and be a real novelty to me, never having made love to a near-corpse."

The sun streamed bright through the windows. The two women were filled with immense good humor, and that good humor spread when Jessica heard the news from Lord Japhe's lips that the English party and Vinegar Varese would ride out of South Pass today. They had had luck.

William Paxton stopped the girl before she could get out of the hotel. "Say," he said, "if you was to make your act a regular attraction, I believe we could both prosper." He licked his lips, and Jessica knew he hoped for more than a business connection.

"No," she said, and brushed on by.

Little Will's horse stood hipshot next to Mountain Jack's tough grulla mustang. Lord Japhe's English saddle looked incongruous on a horse he'd bought from a hostler in Point of Rocks—a horse whose previous owner had worn Crow leggings.

Vinegar Varese didn't care what kind of horse he had, just so it was easy handling and big enough for his bulk. Last summer his horse had pulled an ore wagon, but it was big enough and strong enough to carry his weight.

Jessica hurried by, though horses on the street were quite a novelty. She felt the innocent animals had some important connection to her enemies and might pick up her anxious secrets.

She had reached the ridgetop and was quite out of sight when Little Will strolled onto the boardwalk. Vinegar carried Little Will's saddlebags dangling from each hand. Earlier, he'd packed the horses, though the job had to be redone by Mountain Jack, who cursed Vinegar pretty severely for creating "a packsaddle that'll fall off before we get five miles."

Mountain Jack was ready to go, too—more than ready. He had a ranch to care for. By now he'd quite forgotten the original problem. A little matter of rustlers. He felt like he had unwillingly become the Englishmen's volunteer guide and pack master, and he'd be glad to see the last of them.

Mountain Jack was a mite irritated at Miss Sallie Arthur. This morning, when he'd tiptoed to her room to make apologies and maybe bounce the springs of her bed, she had that damn breed kid posted outside, and he wouldn't let him one step closer, pointing that Hawkins right at his midsection. It was a .50 bore he was looking down, which kind of made up for the kid's youth and lack of experience. Didn't look to be enough room in the hallway for both Mountain Jack and that .50 ball.

So he'd done his explaining through the door, at a shout, so Sallie could hear him. It was mighty embarrassing.

"All I want to do is buy you a cup of coffee, for god's sake. Sallie, open the door! Call off this damn kid!"

She wouldn't call off the kid.

"Sallie, I just want to say goodbye," Jack howled.

"Goodbye. I heard you. Now git!"

Feeling like he'd been kicked for no reason, Mountain Jack followed the others outdoors. He knew he'd be expected to lead the way. Vinegar might know the country better, but he was no horseman. Vinegar was town bred.

Mountain Jack figured they weren't taking any terrible chances. They had four days' rations and enough dry kindling to get a fire going. The whole load was wrapped in a tarp that could do double duty as a tent, and they carried a couple of gallons of clean oats for the horses. They might run across a party of Indians, but they were heavily armed. A bad blizzard could still kill them, but it was spring, and despite his precise precautions, Mountain Jack's heart lifted.

Mountain Jack, then Lord Japhe, then his son and Vinegar Varese and the two packhorses brought up the rear. There wasn't a single soul except William Paxton who was sorry to see them go.

It was easy riding, but they didn't get very far, after all. Around the second bend, where the road skirted the low hillock, they found a horse's leg.

It was stuck in the snow beside the road like a drunken

signpost. The horseshoe glistened in the sunlight. Exposed to the air, it had turned rust-red. Rust so bright it looked like phosphorescent fungus. Mountain Jack got off his horse to see if anything else lay under the snow.

The leg wasn't attached to anything, at least not to a horse. It came away quite readily in his hand.

Little Will's gaze was incurious, Lord Japhe's puzzled. "What do you make of it?" he asked.

"Might be some damn Indian trick." Mountain Jack had one hand on his holster. "But this is a mighty poor place for an ambush."

Lord Japhe shook his head. "Turn it right way up. It looks like it's been cut with a saw. A crude job of butchering."

Mountain Jack said, "There's only one horse in this country we don't know its whereabouts, and that horse is the same color as this."

Little Will took the leg from the dismounted man. "And where the horse is, the rider must be nearby." Will's eyes darted everywhere, feral as a hunting hawk. Without noticing it, he held the leg bone by the haft, like a club.

The snow in all directions was blank and secretive. The ridge slope was unmarked except where it had pulled away from some sun-heated boulder. The nearest trees were across several deer meadows to the west.

"Well, let's be about it," Little Will said excitedly, and kicked his horse off the trail.

Mountain Jack and Lord Japhe stayed still. Vinegar Varese dropped the pack string and jumped his heavy horse up the hill.

The packhorses didn't move. There was no place to go any better than the very spot they stood. Little Will was blundering through the clutching snow. Uphill, Vinegar Varese did the same. Both men were looking for something, and it was Vinegar Varese who found it. Fifty yards up slope, lying almost flat in the snow like a buried branch, was a second leg. He waved it over his head with real enthusiasm. "We get enough of these, we'll have a whole horse," he joked.

Lord Japhe sat quite still. Mountain Jack watched them search while he rolled himself a quirly. He had no taste for this chase, but he had to admit the very peculiarity of the situation appealed to him. What in God's name was a chopped-up horse doing all the way out here in the middle of winter? Mountain Jack's curiosity was fairly intent. He kept an eye on the two men, both quartering the slope above him.

They found the third leg just below the top of the little rise. They never did find the fourth leg. On the far side, down in the gully bottom, the vultures dining on horse flesh were disturbed by all the ruckus and flapped aloft, uttering squeaky complaints.

That was enough for Mountain Jack. He put the spurs to his horse and followed the path created by Little Will and Vinegar Varese.

Lord Japhe waited until all three of his riding partners had dropped out of sight. He extracted his gold hunter. He'd give them ten minutes. If they hadn't returned by then, he'd go back to Paxton's Hotel where he could wait in comfort.

It had taken Lacey Tripp most of a morning and an afternoon to tow the slaughtered horse from the dugout to its separate resting places. The three men retraced his steps in just half an hour and it would have been faster if they hadn't spent so much time trying to figure out what and who. Little Will probed the snow around the horse carcass with his rifle barrel hoping to find Slocum's body.

None of the three spoke. Normally disunited, they were on the trail now and behaved like hunters, accepting Little Will's lead, casting their net wide and wordlessly.

The legs connected to the forequarters. The forequarters were connected to the hindquarters. A straight line. They followed that line out of the second gully, over the wind-blown ridge and down the far side into the pine woods. Here it was tougher going because the snow hadn't melted, so they dismounted and led their horses. Little Will had one hand wrapped in his reins and the other around the butt of his Remington single-action. If they met up with John Slocum in these woods, Will meant to get off the first shot.

No smoke came from the dugout chimney, but there were sounds inside. The noise of somebody walking around— clinking sounds.

They drew up three abreast not twenty feet from the front door. Vinegar had a scattergun across his saddle bow and Mountain Jack drew his pistol.

Because she didn't expect to see anyone, because she was in a hurry, the girl stepped through the door of her cabin without noticing them and turned to attend to the latchstring. She had saddlebags slung over one shoulder.

Some dim remembrance of what she'd seen spun her around again.

"Well, now," Little Will said. "Well, well, well."

Everybody stayed in place until the girl rushed back inside the dugout. Casually, like he had nothing particular in mind, Little Will dismounted and shambled toward the cabin door. Vinegar Varese followed. Vinegar was clutching and unclutching his hands. Mountain Jack ground-reined his horse and gave it a pat before he came along, too.

Little Will stopped over the horse's head beside the cabin door. Little Will touched his hat. "Howdy, partner," he said in an exaggerated westerner's drawl. "I don't suppose you've seen anything of the hombre who rode in on you, did you?" He straightened. "Nope. I reckon not. I guess we'll just have to ask the little lady."

With that he kicked the door right off its leather hinges.

She was inside, in the very back of the dugout, and she had a stove poker.

"Charmin' little place you have here," Little Will said

in his normal voice. "Don't s'pose you been renting out rooms to any cattle rustler named John Slocum, have you?"

Will's eyes glittered. The smile on his face was not very nice.

"Who's he?" she demanded. "You stay back now or I'll crack your skull." She hefted the stove poker like she meant to do just that, but her eyes were desperate, darting here and there.

"You don't have to worry, little girl," Will said, and didn't even bother to disguise the lie in his voice. "We shan't do you any harm."

Vinegar Varese licked his lips. He put on a smile of opportunity. It looked horrible.

Mountain Jack looked all around the cabin but never directly at Jessica.

"I don't suppose you'd like to tell us where you've put him?" Little Will drawled. He removed his hat and set it on the dry sink. He unbuttoned his overcoat. "It'll be a mite chilly in here," he said. "Vinegar, suppose you start a fire. Jack, you go around the cabin and see if there's any sign of our man. I doubt you'll find him, but it'll take a few moments for the cabin to warm."

Jack said sure, sure he would. He made a thorough scout, searching in concentric circles around the cabin, and finding just what he expected: nothing.

The smoke stood in a column above the dugout and the gases and stink drifted over where he was and smelled like hell. When the fire got going good, the smoke diminished to a haze of heat just at the tin chimney mouth.

Mountain Jack heard a scream of pain. Jack leaned against a tree and rolled himself a quirly with his shaking hands. He spilled too much of the tobacco in the snow. Angrily he crumpled the rolling paper into a wad.

He remembered what the girl had looked like. The image of her bare body burned in his mind. In his mind's eye she was bent slightly forward, removing her final piece of clothing from her ankle.

Jessica's howl sounded like the distant howling of a dog.

She wouldn't tell. They'd asked their questions and she wouldn't tell. They didn't care if she talked or not. Jack knew that. Still, he made another tour around the camp, looking for some sign of the man he knew perfectly well wouldn't be there.

What was that sound from inside? A man's laughter? Yes. Little Will and Vinegar Varese were both laughing.

Mountain Jack walked through the snow looking for John Slocum. He kicked at hummocks that wouldn't have concealed a rabbit, let alone a man.

The girl was sobbing. He could hear sobbing quite distinctly.

He stood in the doorway, just like an invited guest. The sobbing was fear and pain and disgust.

He tossed his hat beside Little Will's hat and Vinegar Varese's hat.

The girl was grunting. Sobs and grunts.

Little Will leaned against the wall casually. He had an unlit havana between his teeth. Though he was stripped to the waist and barefoot, he didn't seem to feel the cold. His eyes, as they bored into Jack's, were triumphant. The devil come to collect his due.

"No," the girl said. "No, no!"

Very slowly, Mountain Jack took off his heavy sheepskin coat. He let it fall on the floor.

His hands went to the drawstrings of his buckskin shirt. He was remembering the girl of last night, bent over, graceful as a doe, all sleek lines and shadows.

He was looking at the bottoms of her feet. They were dirty and rough. Her feet, her ankles, her long legs waving in the air, helpless as some kind of insect upended.

And Vinegar Varese's fat white buttocks pumping between those legs. Jack couldn't even see her face, just her black hair.

"Please," she said. "Please. No."

"You can go next," Little Will whispered. What a smile he had.

"I've done some bad things in my life," Jack said.

Little Will grinned at him. The sound from the narrow cot was awful. Her arms fluttered helplessly. Her legs waved helplessly.

Jack set the door back in place so nobody could see.

9

They had good luck with the trains. That spring, until May, train service in the far west was extremely erratic. Sometimes the U.P. got through, sometimes they didn't; but it wasn't any trouble for Lord Japhe, Vinegar Varese, Mountain Jack, and Little Will.

The men never said a word about the Indian girl, not even to each other. They hurried back into South Pass long enough to chivvy the English lord into travel. Then they rode all day and later than it was wise to ride at all. They made a cold camp and the three younger men took turns standing watch. They told Lord Japhe they were worried about the Indians. He just looked at them, never said a thing.

Nobody paid them any attention when they rode into Point of Rocks, right down the center of the muddy main street.

It was the worse season for railroad builders—unstable mud, unstable slush. Some engineers joked that they would have preferred ice—any form that stayed stable.

Mud-covered laborers, tracklayers, and engineers reeled

through the streets between work and bed, work and food, or work and work. They didn't pay so much attention to the girls or the gambling or the booze, though they'd turn to those amusements soon enough. With the return of summer colors and summer strength, a hard day's work would seem like nothing more than preparation for a hard night's play. They were young men, in their prime, and could take anything anyone handed to them.

The four mud-spattered riders hurried straight through Point of Rocks and had only an hour to wait for the eastbound. They'd have to ride an empty immigrant train, but they didn't care. They were in a hurry.

On the station platform Lord Japhe fired a havana and said to Mountain Jack, "I wish we could have brought Jessica Tripp out with us. That young girl deserves an education."

"I imagine," Mountain Jack mumbled, running his jacket fringe through his calloused hands.

"Oh, she'll get education enough," Little Will said.

Vinegar Varese laughed right on cue.

The cars smelled funny. Too many unwashed human bodies, traveling too fast across the nation, in a hurry to reach the jumping-off point before they ran out of money.

The floors were splotched with chewing tobacco and dirt. In one corner a bundle of diapers lay. They didn't bear inspecting too closely.

The windows were smudged and the heat in the car wasn't very good because they didn't use the new cars for the immigrant trains.

Lord Japhe sat at one end of the car. The other men occupied the other end. None of them had a taste for cards to while away the time, though Little Will suggested a friendly game. All of them had bottles and they worked on them. It was the only tribute the three ever paid the young girl, getting wobbly drunk on the train between Point of Rocks and Cheyenne.

Lord Japhe was paying all their fares, and when he announced his decision to stay overnight in Cheyenne and catch the first passenger train next day they agreed, though Little Will and Vinegar wanted to get as far as possible as fast as possible.

That night, drinking at a back table in the Silver Dollar Saloon, Mountain Jack said, "I reckon I'll go back East with you. There's boys on the place who can take care of the Swan Ranch."

"Surely," Will said, and smiled. "Be pleased to have you come along."

"Can't stay here," Mountain Jack said to his whiskey glass. He emptied it and poured himself another. His hands were trembling.

"She was just a half-breed," Little Will said. "We didn't take a thing from her she won't be selling tomorrow. And we paid her, didn't we? We paid her fifty dollars. Now, what breed commands that kind of price? Man, don't be dim."

"If I stayed out here," Jack said, "no decent man would have nothing to do with me. Likely somebody'd blow my head off one day just from annoyance. There ain't so many whites out here, and word gets around. This chase of ours—why, it'll be saloon gossip by spring from here to Butte City. Sallie Arthur told me some things about this Slocum fellow. He may have done a few things in his time that weren't sanctioned by the Good Book, but he's a man to ride the river with. Us? I don't reckon we'll be thought well of in the territories. Not after what we done."

Irritated, Will said, "Fine," and sneered. "Since you've quit your employ at the Swan Ranch, I suggest I hire you as my conscience."

Mountain Jack lowered his head. "I surely wish you gents hadn't come riding by last fall. I surely wish that. None of this would have happened."

"Oh, my," Little Will said. "It's going to be such a *long* journey."

He was wrong. Next morning they jumped aboard the

U.P.'s eastbound and Lord Japhe retired to a green wingback chair in the parlor car. They had a fair assortment of magazines there, none more than two months old, and Lord Japhe lost himself in the history and personalities of his times. He drank no more than usual, just a glass before lunch and another before his supper. The train hurtled east. Sometimes the great plains were clear and white for miles. Sometimes the train thundered above mud-swelled streams or between great high snow walls.

They didn't see much alive. Once, down in a river bottom already green-yellow, they saw some pronghorns grazing and there were great flights of birds overhead. But the image persisted of a dead, lifeless landscape, unfit for humankind.

Cheyenne to Omaha. They stopped at every little way station and men got on or off. Generally, the train was pretty full. But no matter how full it got, nobody argued when Vinegar Varese sprawled his bulk across two seats and rested his muddy boots on a third. Men stood, ladies too, but nobody pestered him.

Vinegar had taken to keeping his ash cudgel lying across his lap, three feet of sweat-darkened wood. It looked like just what it was: a deadly weapon.

And Vinegar Varese was in quite a temper. The parlor steward had asked Little Will to keep his servant back with the poorer passengers because his countenance disturbed the quality folk.

With a big laugh, Little Will said, "Surely. His face does wear on a man."

So Vinegar Varese was exiled to the common car while the others sat in plush lounge chairs drowning their sorrows with high-quality booze.

It wasn't the first time Vinegar Varese had been excluded on account of his terrible face. But he had hoped teaming up with Little Will would put an end to that experience.

Vinegar Varese had begun to put some faith in Little Will. Vinegar hoped his luck had changed. He was delighted when Little Will dropped his drawers in that chilly soddy to be first with that half-breed girl. When Vinegar went second, it sealed their accord, or so he thought. Finding himself excluded from the company eroded at Vinegar Varese's confidence as his teeth chewed flecks from his lower lip. He mumbled, too, and stroked the ash cudgel.

No wonder nobody wanted to take the seat next to him or across, or even the vacant seat next to the place taken up by his boots.

In the sumptuous parlor car, Little Will flipped the cards one at a time for solataire.

"I don't see how you can enjoy a game like that when you cheat all the time," Mountain Jack observed.

"Why don't you ask the attendant to bring me another brandy and soda?" Little Will murmured.

"It just ain't no kind of a challenge when you play it that way," Mountain Jack insisted.

"I make my own rules. Brandy and soda, please?"

Mountain Jack did as he was told, brought Little Will's drink and a stiff one for himself. He never would have thought to be drinking such good whiskey. He never thought it would taste so bad..

Mountain Jack sat in a chair nearest the window and turned it so it faced out. He rested his boot heels on the mahogany paneling. The drawn curtains were green velvet fringed with little velvet knots.

Mountain Jack watched the varying flow of the landscape without seeing anything particular. His gaze was locked within.

Her skin had been so soft, soft as the down of a baby dove. How had he raped her? How had it happened? He could have turned at the door, but he had fastened the door on its hinges, and in the dim light streaming through that single glass window, in that chilly dugout, he'd taken the sobbing, pained girl.

Maybe he was one of those men who had to destroy anything they found beautiful. Maybe that was how things made him act. Thoughts like these went through Mountain

Jack's mind because, not being the sort of man to kill himself, he would have to live what remained of his life with some understanding of the creature he had become.

He had ruined his life. He knew that perfectly well. He'd played cards he never should have drawn and though he'd won the pot, he'd lost his life. So now what?

Mountain Jack was reassessing his own image of himself downward. He'd always known he had courage and some cunning and just enough horse sense to get by in the hard country, but those virtues weren't enough. He'd had enough pure craziness in him to rape a beautiful girl, and everything had changed. Mountain Jack felt like a man who suddenly changed sides in the midst of a war. It could be done, but it was a wrench, and took a little getting used to.

And somehow he'd found himself attached to Little Will Japhe. Wasn't that a surprise?

How had he fallen so far? Maybe that was why Sallie Arthur kicked him out of her room that morning, because she'd seen Mountain Jack's future written in his face. Mountain Jack thought about that notion for a while and then began to get another notion. Maybe there was some other reason Sallie Arthur wanted him out of her room. She and those half-breed kids were always hanging around together, Sallie acting like she was some sort of teacher instead of what she was, which was no better than she should be. Sallie and the half-breeds and John Slocum. That idea grew in Mountain Jack's mind like the idea was a living thing, until it just filled up his whole skull.

Now he understood why Sallie Arthur had turned on him. It was because she meant to hide somebody in her room. John Slocum.

For some reason, putting the puzzle together cheered Mountain Jack up quite a bit. The trick played on him had the effect of making him feel less bad about what the three of them had done to Jessica Tripp. Mountain Jack became so excited that he went over to Lord Japhe's chair and hunkered down before him and told him his deduction: that Jessica Tripp had served as a decoy while the others smuggled their quarry to safety.

Lord Japhe took a sip of whiskey. "I see," he said. He even smiled for the first time since they'd hurried him out of South Pass. "When that child came down the stairs to perform her act in Paxton's saloon, I knew I was escorting an accomplished woman. I had no idea *how* accomplished. Tell me, Jack, just what did you three find that day? You remember, when you split off after the horse parts? Did you find more horse parts? What else did you find? My son has grown unaccustomed to confiding in me, and his brute won't. Can I count on you for the truth?"

Jack flushed to the roots of his hair and wouldn't meet the man's eyes. "No, sir. I don't believe I can talk about that," he said.

Lord Japhe's face went all cold again and he nodded shortly. "I see," he said. And maybe he did see.

It took the little pleasure right out of Mountain Jack's mouth, turned it sour, and put that pleasure away like a tainted sweet. What they had done was unforgivable. No more than that. And because he, of all of them, had the most sense, it was more his responsibility than the others'.

Thus Mountain Jack passed the time between Cheyenne and Omaha. In Omaha they caught the St. Louis train.

At the St. Louis Union Station, Lord Japhe descended the stairs painfully. He stood on the busy boards of the platform watching the bustle, the steam of locomotives, warning bells, the clatter of hand trucks and porters' calls.

"Father," Little Will said, "if we don't purchase tickets, we will be unable to continue our journey east."

"They call St. Louis the gateway to the West," Lord Japhe mused.

"Yes." Little Will spoke impatiently. "Gateway to the West. That's what they told us last time we passed through. The tickets, Father."

His father didn't seem to get the point. He smiled vaguely. "I'll rest here for a bit," he said. He rubbed his legs. "Old joints, you know," he said vaguely.

"Perhaps we shall go on ahead," Little Will said through gritted teeth.

"As you like," his lordship said vaguely.

"We shall need some money for tickets and expenses," Little Will said through his teeth. "I find myself temporarily embarrassed. . . ."

"Money?" His father put an idiot's smile on his face. "I told you you will have a lump sum settlement. You shall have it in London, if you like."

"How about St. Louis?" Little Will snapped.

"Oh, I don't think so. St. Louis is so far away. I'll cable my agents and see what can be done."

"I suppose that'll have to do."

Lord Japhe had moved shipments by elephant through India. He had directed the movement of trading schooners along the Madagascar coast. He had provisioned war expeditions. It was perhaps odd that he was quite unable to transfer Little Will's inheritance from London to St. Louis.

Little Will lacked for nothing, of course. Nothing but freedom.

He, Vinegar, and Mountain Jack were installed in a floor of the River House. Each had his own bedroom, and their sitting room was opulent by frontier standards: three horsehair couches, a secretary, a rug, and beside each couch, a wrought iron floor-standing ashtray.

Lord Japhe took a spartan room on the next floor in the very back of the hotel. The management offered him a suite but his lordship declined their offer, preferring the consolations of his monkish room and his Bible. He concentrated his reading on the New Testament, seeking some proof of a redemption that suited him.

Lord Japhe paid all the bills. Hotel bills, restaurant bills, bills from the clothiers all three of the other men frequented. Vinegar Varese bought himself a suit of beetle-shell green.

He bought a buffalo hunter's leather sombrero to go with it and a pair of white boots that were a trifle too small for him and pinched his feet. He had a gold nubbin put on the small tip of his cudgel and carried the deadly instrument the way a gentleman carries a cane.

Mountain Jack was fitted for several businesman's suits. Mountain Jack asked the tailor to make the suits like those boilerplate suits Pinkerton Agents often wore. He selected this style not because he admired the Pinkertons but precisely because he didn't. The tailor did his best fitting the rough Westerner, but succeeded only in creating a twisted, oddly shaped figure. Mountain Jack had worn buckskins for twenty years. He tied his buckskins up with his fringed belt and dropped the bundle into the river. Mountain Jack dropped his medicine bag in the river, too.

He was pretty drunk standing on the wharf watching a white steamboat chuffing up river and the bubbles of air from the bottom. He sighed as he said goodbye to the man he'd been.

Little Will was unsatisfied. Though he'd enjoyed St. Louis on the way west, the city held few charms for him now. The tailors he employed so frequently were, he said, inferior to London tailors. And, of course, he didn't care for his accommodations, right next to the river with its constant traffic, its freight, its steam whistles, men hurrying to and fro at all hours of the day and night.

Little Will found St. Louis society banal and said so. He also wondered loudly why his money had not yet arrived to set him free.

Lord Japhe could not or would not enlighten him on this point and became, in fact, rather illusive, choosing to take meals in his room and refusing to open the door despite the lengthiest and most sorrowful entreaties from his son.

He paid all the bills, but that was all he paid. Little Will tried to get ready cash by a trick. He asked one of his tailors to pad the bill to the tune of several thousand, promising to split the extra with the tailor. But Lord Japhe must have scented something wrong, because he didn't pay that man's bill. Not the padded bill nor the legitimate bill, either, despite repeated requests.

Lord Japhe stayed in his room until the very early hours of the morning. First light often found him, impeccably dressed, strolling the wharves, watching the river flow south.

During the War St. Louis had been Yankee but many of her citizens were sympathizers of the Confederate cause. Johnny Rebs had almost captured the St. Louis arsenal and twice confederate expeditions had been mounted to take the town. The Unionists were Germans and midwesterners. The Southern sympathizers were of Scotch-Irish extraction, a fact they often boasted about.

St. Louis had been fur capital of the world for many years and St. Louis society reflected that, too. There were three different aristocracies in St. Louis in 1869. The German-Yankee brewers and merchants, prosperous, optimistic, perhaps a little rough and ready; the Southern aristocracy, deprived of slaves and rather impoverished but exquisitely mannered; and a few fur families like the Astors who traveled between St. Louis and Manhattan. These last were generally acknowledged to be the top of the heap, and these families knew Little Will Japhe and his peculiar associates but didn't recognize them. The other branches of high society weren't quite so particular. The Southerners saw Little Will as "one of their kind" and the Germans saw him as a "fine sort of a chap. Level-headed, too."

Everybody was very curious about Lord Japhe, and Little Will had to invent stories to explain his non-appearance. Some of these stories were quite ingenious, but none of them was particularly consistent.

Little Will went horse racing. He bought a fine standard bred and raced him in on the green tracks of the course north of town. He went on picnics, he attended socials. He accepted invitations to grand balls. When it amused him, he brought Vinegar Varese along at his side, as his man-servant. Vinegar Varese was always eager to accompany Little Will and sulked when he was left alone at home.

Mountain Jack didn't care much one way or another. For weeks he stayed in the River House saloon, drinking from sunup to sundown.

To replace his belted revolvers, he'd invested in a snub-nosed Colt .44 caliber. Every afternoon he'd interrupt his drinking for a long session shooting beer bottles on the riverbank. Every day he burned two or three hundred rounds, the Colt appearing in his hand like greased lightning.

Then he'd return to the saloon, cleaning his revolver right at the table he'd established as his own.

April was cold and wet, May sunny and warm. The social whirl of St. Louis went into high gear and Little Will attended one gala after another. Many socialites were flattered by his stylish presence at their affairs.

Little Will was charming. His jibes and jests, his sneers and almost-insults were taken as evidence of wit and superior breeding. He was "doing the tour," he told them. He didn't once mention his father. Will had not been in Lord Japhe's presence for two weeks.

The tall grass and balmy air of early June. Hearing no more about his money, Little Will became desperate. Did his father mean for him to rot right here? Mountain Jack was already rotting, and Little Will was feeling the pressure. So long as he was allowed to accompany his master, Vinegar Varese was content—the only contented man among them.

Finally, Little Will hit on a scheme. His father had always enjoyed formal balls, and he'd always liked to see his son well approved in society. Little Will would throw a ball.

Will had gotten to know the younger fellows in St. Louis society and he consulted them as to the best way to do it.

A ballroom was engaged at the regimental armory. Gangs of workmen repainted the place and polished and waxed the lovely hardwood floor. St. Louis was searched for a proper band. So soon after the war, music was still politically charged, and brawls broke out at the playing of the "Battle Hymn of the Republic" or "Dixie." The suitable band turned out to be a German brass band with a small string ensemble who would saw away at waltzes while their counterparts rested their horns on their laps.

Newspaper announcements described the event to those fortunate to have invitations as well as those who had none. The Stars and Stripes and the Union Jack were draped as bunting from cornices on the armory windows.

To honor Lord Japhe, formerly of the East India Company, was how the event was described.

Two weeks before the event, still without talking to Little Will, Lord Japhe sent out for a tailor and had him make up a new set of formal wear. Will, who bribed the tailor for details, was delighted. He went ahead with his preparations. Since he knew that Mountain Jack and Vinegar Varese reminded Lord Japhe of certain unpleasantnesses, Little Will specifically told them not to come.

And Little Will's happiness was assured when one of the Astors, who had been invited as a matter of course, returned an invitation with the scribbled note: "Certainly we'll come. We'd love to meet your father again."

Everything was working fine. Little Will, always a dandy, took particular care with his clothing that night. It took him fifteen minutes to decide on shirt studs.

The evening was balmy, the river smell sweeter than usual, and flowers bloomed in the tubs outside the River House where Little Will waited for his handsome coach. He plucked a single blossom for his jacket front.

Fashionably late, Little Will Japhe swept into the ballroom. The brass players got to their feet and blew a salute.

It was, by all accounts, the most important affair of the season. Loafers waited on the sidewalk and small children cheered invited guests as they arrived. Most everybody who had received an invitation came, and everyone wore his fanciest garb. The sparkle of laughter, the gleam of jewels, breasts daringly clad in swooping decolletage.

At ten o'clock the Astor party arrived and sought out Little Will.

Astor himself, magnate of the fur trade, deigned to shake Little Will's hand. "Know your father," the gray-haired merchant king said. "Always liked him. When do you expect his lordship to arrive?"

"Any moment now, sir," Little Will said. He couldn't have been wronger.

Little Will hoped this evening would set the stage for a reconciliation with his father. Though Will set no great store by his father's love, he counted on the money he so desperately wanted. Give him his inheritance and he'd be shut of this grubby American hamlet for the capitals of Europe. Little Will had great hopes.

Ten-thirty rolled around, then eleven. The dancing continued happily. Some guests explained to other guests that English custom was different from American and very often guests of honor, if they were Englishmen, didn't arrive until midnight. And, besides, the snooty Astors were here, weren't they?

At the stroke of midnight he still hadn't come. A few minutes later the Astors and their entourage swept out. By one o'clock most of St. Louis' prominent citizens had left and by two only the avid social climbers remained at Little Will's ball. The band played on. Some danced, many stood and talked. Many cast glances at Little Will, who was hitting the champagne punch pretty hard. At three o'clock Little Will went over to the prettiest girl left at the ball, Miss Rebecca Saunders, and asked for a dance. Rather reluctantly, Miss Saunders agreed to his request. "Just one, sir, and then I must leave. My fiancé is waiting for me outside in his carriage."

Nobody knew what prompted Little Will. As he danced,

he danced faster and faster, quite wildly, like some mad Russian hussar. The unfortunate Rebecca was forced to accompany him, swinging faster than she had ever danced before.

Their motion was so precipitous that it forced other dancers off the floor.

The music rose to new heights and some of the musicians, seeing their employer in a frenzy, sawed louder. Two horn players rose to their feet and blew their trumpets, creating a noise that might have awakened the dead.

At the close of the dance, Rebecca's face was wet with perspiration, Little Will's cruel jaw was white and cold. He sneered his "thank you." He asked, in a voice loud enough to penetrate the farthest reaches of the hall, whether she would accompany him to his hotel for dalliance. "I'll make it worth your while," he said. "Last wench I bedded got fifty dollars for a few minutes' work."

Miss Saunders fainted. There were shocked gasps. Miss Saunders's companions surrounded her unconscious but outraged form and hurried her outdoors, where the air was more salubrious.

Everybody followed. And nobody thanked Little Will for the party, not even the musicians, who sent their bill directly to Lord Japhe.

Rebecca's fiancé sent Little Will a stiff note demanding an apology or he would face the consequences.

"Damn you, too," Little Will said, and cleaned his pistols.

Accompanied by Vinegar Varese and Mountain Jack, Little Will met the aggrieved fiancé next day on the same race course they had visited before in happier circumstances.

The fiancé renewed his demand for an apology. Little Will said something quite rude, and moments later shot out the fiancé's right eye, causing Rebecca to faint once again, a swoon she was slow to come out of.

That tore it. Polite society closed its doors on the man

they were beginning to call "the disgraceful Englishman." No more fetes or galas, no balls or sculling on the river, no well-bred women.

Well, as Little Will was heard to say, there's more than one society. And he was likely right, too.

If they couldn't enjoy the respect of St. Louis' high society then the low would do quite as well. With the riffraff, Little Will was soon very much at home.

Vinegar Varese couldn't have been happier. Now he could accompany his boss everywhere, into every low dive and bucket shop along the river. They went out every night at 9:00 P.M. and generally crawled back at dawn.

Lord Japhe didn't seem to care. He payed their bills at the gin mills as readily as he'd paid the rent for the formal ballroom. But he never told Little Will about the money he awaited; no information at all.

Their evenings were "sport." That was Little Will's word. It was sport to drink themselves into insensibility. Sport to wake in the ditch beside some distant toll road with pockets turned out and no idea how to get home.

It was sport to find the men who'd robbed them. More sport to track them to their own favorite den. More sport when Vinegar Varese beat one man's skull into a pulp with his cudgel while Mountain Jack covered the others with his hideout Colt.

Jack was so quick with that pistol that the worst ruffians froze while one of their number suffered a particularly grisly death.

Vinegar kept pounding the man long after there was no need for another blow, long after the slack body bounced on the hard dirt floor of that saloon as lively as a rag doll.

That was sport. It was sport in the brothels. One memorable night Vinegar, Mountain Jack, and Little Will hired the Lovelight and all its girls. They closed all the blinds to the Lovelight's big parlor so nobody but they and the women would ever know what went on. They kept the Lovelight a private party for three day and took every girl in every available aperture, sometimes two or three on the same girl. They favored the youngest girls, sixteen-year-old whores, and when they finished at the Lovelight they tried to smuggle two girls into the River House.

It was difficult on a Monday at high noon. The clerk and several special constables refused them the stairs. One constable held a staff every bit as long as Vinegar Varese's weapon and another had a scattergun cocked and leveled. The clerk explained, "Women of this type aren't allowed at the River House, sir. No doubt there are other hotels down the street that would be glad to accommodate you." Even backed by two constables and one scattergun, the clerk didn't risk a huge sneer, just a little one.

The clerk was right, too. The three men and two girls found a room right away in another hotel down the river, nearer Steamboat Row. Vinegar Varese removed the connecting door in their suite. He particularly enjoyed screwing one of the girls as soon as Little Will Japhe was done with her.

Mountain Jack didn't change his suit any more. Though he had three perfectly clean suits, he seemed to prefer one gray pin-stripe with a torn pant cuff and a greasy streak under his lapel where his hand dived for his pistol during pistol practice.

Precisely at noon every day, no matter what, Mountain Jack walked down to the river for another practice session. It was as if the pistol practice was a talisman—his only connection with reality.

Little Will prowled the wharves. He sought out trouble, and in that part of the city trouble wasn't hard to find. In June he fought two duels, in the first week of July another one. One of the duels was an old-fashioned handkerchief duel. Two men grip a handkerchief in their teeth. Both hold twelve-inch Bowie knives. If anyone releases the handkerchief, the spectators shoot him dead. Little Will gutted his man. Vinegar Varese called his approval from the edge of the crowd. Most of the crowd was disappointed because Little Will and his pals were too rough and a bit too lucky for their tastes.

The gutted corpse lay on the floor until the swamper dragged it over against the far wall. When the joint cleared out at dawn, they'd toss the man through the trap door into the river. Let the fish have him.

Men drank and discussed the fight. Little Will sat at the bar and accepted congratulations. The air was rank with whiskey, tobacco and kerosene smoke blurred faces and made shapes indistinct.

Vinegar Varese, momentarily sobered by Little Will's victory, had drunk nearly a bottle of whiskey since noon the previous day. Vinegar didn't quite trust his own senses. He squinted, trying to peer through the smoke.

That face.

Those dark dark eyes staring at him from the far side of the room—some friend of Little Will's victim? Someone from another saloon?

The giant shook his head to clear the fumes and when he opened his eyes again, the face had vanished. That face should have meant something to him. Maybe just a dream. Despite the absence of the face, despite his growing conviction that he'd just suffered a waking nightmare, Vinegar Varese got to his feet and shambled across the room. If he confronted the nightmare, it couldn't hurt him. Certainly not that half-breed kid.

What did they call him? Lacey. Funny sort of a name. Vinegar Varese didn't want to remember the half-breed's sister, so he didn't.

Vinegar slipped outside where the horses were hitched. His hand was wrapped around his cudgel, and God help the living brain that club encountered. Vinegar searched the faces of men outside in that morning and even the faces of the drunks passed out in the mire. "Nobody had come that way. What was his trouble, eh? Ghosts?" Raucous laughter.

And Vinegar stood beside the door of that waterfront dive and no man passed outside without him looking in his face. None of the faces belonged to the half-breed boy.

Just a bad turn. Somebody walking over his grave. That's how Vinegar Varese came to think of it when he sobered up. And he vowed to stay away from the Triple X poison that was ruining him. That night, as the cab horses were steaming and stamping, Vinegar Varese called to his driver, "Stop! Stop man!" and hurtled his great body into the fog, abandoning Little Will, dashing beneath steel hooves, seeking the face he'd glimpsed from the carriage.

Vinegar Varese came up empty though he dragged several men into the light to examine them and made few friends.

Shivering, a nervous Vinegar Varese wouldn't touch a drop of whiskey that night or the next. This abstinence rather annoyed Little Will, who conversed only with Mountain Jack and humiliated his manservant at every opportunity.

Vinegar's nerves calmed the very next morning, which happened to be a Sunday. Waking at an unusually early hour, Vinegar Varese encountered Lord Japhe entering a carriage for hire.

"I am going to St. Stephen's," his lordship told the brute. And, indeed, the nobleman had a prayer book in his hand.

"Sure," Vinegar Varese said. "Sure..."

St. Stephen's was almost as old as St. Louis Cathedral and quite crowded even at the early morning service. Many people knew Lord Japhe only by sight since he arrived late, departed quickly, and rarely spoke. Heads turned when the nobleman took his usual pew. The man beside him was so terribly scarred he looked more like some poor ape than a man.

Lord Japhe slipped smoothly into the ritual.

The service was, as usual, quiet and a balm to the heart until, midway through the choir anthem, Lord Japhe's companion jumped to his feet, stabbed a finger at the choir stall, and shrieked, "You! I'll kill you, you son of a bitch ghost!" He started for the back exit that led to the stalls. It took the efforts of four ushers to restrain him and he finally grew silent only when rapped smartly by one usher's ecclesiastical cosh.

Vinegar Varese woke beside the steps of the church with an ache in his head an the indelible memory of the two half-breeds, the boy and the girl, singing in that church choir. Ghosts. He was being haunted by ghosts, no doubt. He sought comfort down by the riverfront, finding peace in the bottles he emptied that night and the next. He drank until he could not stand and then he drank on his knees until he couldn't drink that way. He fell into the sawdust and the two men who robbed him cracked his ribs with their boot toes because they meant to uphold the honor of the fair city of St. Louis which this ugly man and the English lordling had sullied.

Vinegar Varese woke with other drunks beside the river bank. He woke when a rat ran over his face. Vinegar stifled a shriek. They'd been wagoneered out to this spot from half a dozen riverside dives and not a man of them hadn't been cleaned before being dropped among the bullrushes and cattails. Somebody near the bottom of the pile rolled so his face was in shallow water and while Varese watched, indifferent, the man inhaled water, sputtered, inhaled again, and drowned in six inches of water.

Fog was swirling like black smoke. Either it was morning or late dusk, one or the other. A loon called from the river, a high, crazy cry. Vinegar Varese held his rotten head and reflected that life had cheated him.

Footsteps coming down the riverbank, steady, one pair. Directly Vinegar Varese could make out the face he gasped "YOU!" and choked his cudgel closer. His cudgel was all the thieves had left to him. It was too ugly to steal, though one of the thieves had pried the little gold tip off the end of the wood.

The half-breed had grown taller since the last time Varese

saw him. Vinegar Varese wet his lips. "How?" he asked.

Lacey Tripp looked at the man. Vinegar's shirt-front was covered with river mud and other fluids less describable. His hair was wild, his eyes pure pain. His strong hands trembled. His slack jaw hung half open and drool dribbled from the corner of his mouth.

Lacey Tripp smiled. "Come," he said, "I will do you a great favor."

Without another word, the half-breed turned on his heels into the fog bank whence he'd come.

Shivering from head to foot, Vinegar Varese stumbled to his feet and reeled in pursuit. The boy was shadow in the mist and though he pushed himself into a painful, drunken half-run, the boy kept an easy lead.

They hurried along rough muddy roads, Vinegar falling to his knees again and again in the mud. Once he slipped sideways into the roadside ditch. Every time he fell the boy paused, and every time the man got back to his feet the shadow fled again, just ahead of him.

Vinegar ran hard, tongue lolling out of his mouth, his breath searing and rasping past his lips. His head pounded and he ran through a haze of his own thudding blood. His stomach was on some other planet and his brain was as thin as a shaved dime.

He ran for ten minutes, a half hour, like some poor damned soul perpetually seeking that which ruins him.

The chase stopped at the River House. Men were coming and going from that familiar establishment and none paid any attention to the well dressed dark-complexioned boy or the mud-covered savage who pursued him.

John Slocum sat in the open doorway of a handsome carriage and Jessica Tripp, dressed quite elegantly, sat on the seat behind him.

"As you can see," John Slocum said, closing his clasp knife and pocketing his whittling, "we have come for satisfaction."

The boy Lacey had one hand in his jacket pocket. He was wearing the worst face Vinegar Varese had ever seen.

Lightly, John Slocum dropped onto the street. A couple drummers hurried into the River House, lost in the details of their business deal. They didn't notice a thing.

The tall green-eyed man wore a three-piece suit with a broad collar and a Western flare. His dark plainsman's hat was impeccable. When he brushed his coat aside, Vinegar Varese saw the ebony-handled Colt strapped to the thigh. "Mr. Varese," John Slocum said calmly, "do you have any last words?"

"Aw, shit. Aw, shit!"

Those last words did as well as any.

10

When Jessica Tripp's worried brother came out to the dugout seeking her, she was just feeding the last pieces of the bed into the fire. She was so sore that she walked bowlegged. Her arms and one of her knees were bruised purple. One eye was black and swollen shut. She was crawling on the floor when Lacey found her, but she insisted on feeding the last piece of that bed into the fire before she'd go with him to Sallie Arthur's and comfort.

Directly, John Slocum got his pins under him. A tall, laconic, quiet man, he ate carefully and often, exercised as best he could, and as soon as he was able, took to the streets of South Pass to build up his strength.

The miners understood that Slocum was the man they'd hunted but they'd altered their sympathies considerably when they learned of the group rape. Many of the miners were a little bit in love with the girl who'd revealed herself that memorable evening, and it was a good thing the English party had left town when it did. John Slocum got civil greetings and some curious questions, all of which he ignored with the same calm, sad expression. At first, when he walked from one end of South Pass's main street to the other, he hurt. He favored his wound and kind of walked

171

funny. He straightened as he grew stronger.

Jessica Tripp lay in Sallie's room, eating hardly a thing, as her bruises healed.

It wasn't the end of the winter. There were still snowfalls to come. But Slocum was spending most of his days outdoors, in the hills. One sunny day he walked down the street with a Colt Navy on his hip and extra ammunition wrapped in his jacket.

After that, the crack of gunfire in the woods came to be as common a sound as the rushing of the sluice waters or Major Wright's blasting powder. The Major freighted in his new seven-stamp mill. It was a wonder.

Jessica Tripp answered every question Sallie Arthur asked her in the same grave tone. She rarely started any conversations herself, and she usually kept the blinds drawn.

Lacey Tripp continued his work for William Paxton, but he boiled with a sullen rage, and most of Paxton's customers gave the Indian kid a wide birth.

Late in May, John Slocum stamped into Sallie Arthur's room and flipped the blinds open. Jessica Tripp threw her hands over her eyes. "That hurts," she whimpered.

"Get out of bed," the tall man said. "We're going after them."

During Jessica's long rest, Lacey Tripp had often dreamed of doing just that.

"We're gonna set your feet right," he said. "We're gonna line you up for an education."

Jessica didn't care so much about that as she once had, but she got out of bed.

"Cover yourself," Slocum said, throwing her a robe. "You ain't no two-bit whore."

Surprised, the girl did as she was told.

John Slocum was healthy as he'd ever been, with just one more scar on his body to remind him of where he'd been. His face was pretty pale but the callouses were hard on his hammer thumb.

South Pass had opened up again. Everybody understood it would close down next winter and only diehards still thought they were going to hit the mother lode here. But, no matter, it was spring, and men meant to do the best they could.

One fine morning, John Slocum, Lacey, and Jessica climbed aboard the Point of Rocks stage. They didn't have very much luggage. Slocum said they'd get some gear when they hit Cheyenne.

A tearful Sallie Arthur saw them off. She hated to see the kids go, though having them in her room all the time had somewhat cramped her style.

She'd taken a real shine to Slocum, too, though he never gave her a play. He always treated her like a lady; that's what she liked about him. Sallie was both pleased and displeased. Pleased because she knew Slocum and Mountain Jack were enemies, and she didn't care to sleep with her ex-lover's enemy. Displeased because she suspected he'd be fun in the sack. "I guess you're still pretty tired," she said, and slugged his arm.

He gave her a wan grin. "Sallie, I been shot and chased and a little girl got raped because she wouldn't tell my enemies where I was. I don't figure I got a right to do anything I'd like until I wipe the slate clean."

"Yeah," she'd said. "That's what I meant."

So now she stood in the dusty street of South Pass and the impossible sky reeled overhead and the two half-breeds boarded the coach and John Slocum was tipping his hat to her from beside the driver on the box. Sallie didn't think she'd ever forget his face or how Jessica looked, sitting pressed against the side of the coach, sad and pale. Sometimes life was like that.

The driver kicked the footbrake and popped his reins and yelled "Haw!" and Sallie Arthur trudged back into Paxton's hotel, wearier than she had ever been. She hoped Jessica would write once she reached her destination.

They entrained that evening. The boy was fascinated by the railroad—he'd never seen one before—but Jessica was silent as a prisoner.

The next morning, in Cheyenne, John Slocum took both of them around to a tailor's and dressmaker's and outfitted them for their journey. He bought a good pair of boots for himself and boots for the boy, too.

Jessica showed no particular interest in the dresses the clerk held up to her. Finally, John Slocum said. "I want her well dressed for travel and meeting some important people. Six outfits ought to do it. If she don't care, I do. You dress her how you see fit and pack the dresses in a trunk."

They stayed in the Drover House and Slocum and Lacey Tripp ate a fine dinner. Jessica's cheeks were very hollow. She just picked at her food. Slocum asked a few questions at the hotel and down at the depot. If the English party hadn't been among the very first to come out in the spring, they might have been harder to remember. For some reason, people remembered Little Will. They remembered him in Omaha, too.

This far east, and considerably south, spring was well advanced. The days were warmer and the nights were rarely chilly. Jessica ate, slept, and kept her own counsel. John Slocum let her be until he took a good suite of rooms in St. Louis. He'd elected a new hotel, to the north, five miles outside of St. Louis proper. Slocum didn't want to cross paths with the Englishman until he had a few other jobs done.

He hired watches to keep a loose eye on Little Will. Particularly he wanted to know if the party suddenly showed signs of traveling on.

He sought interviews with several of St. Louis' most important bankers. These bankers were quite willing to oblige Mr. J. Slocum. News of his wealth had traveled and bankers were quite willing to oblige Mr. Slocum so long as his deposits were large.

Once he'd talked to the bankers, he visited with the reverends, deacons, preachers, and monsignors of St. Louis' most prominent churches. When he had learned everything he could, John Slocum made an appointment to see Miss Parker's School for Young Ladies.

"I don't care if she learns good manners," Slocum said. "That ain't the purpose of her education. She's to learn writing and mathematics."

Miss Parker took a longer look at John Slocum. A Westerner from his look, and a Southerner before that. She fussed with her spectacles like she didn't know whether to wear them or not. Finally she laid the spectacles on her polished desk. "Mr. Slocum," she said slowly, "at this point in time, there isn't so very much a woman can do except acquire manners. You say your niece has studied the Bard. Shakespeare is all well and good, but such knowledge does not guarantee a woman a place in what is, I fear, a man's world. I applaud your decision to place Jessica here in my school, but I would not wish to give you false hopes. We shall teach your niece manners, Mr. Slocum. They may be her most useful tool."

"I heard you were the best girls' school in St. Louis." Slocum said. "You graduated from a man's college, didn't you?"

"I was allowed to attend Cornell," Miss Parker admitted. "A canvas screen divided my seat from the seats of the male students. The school feared my presence would distract them."

"That's crazy."

"Yes, sir, it is. It is also the way of the world. Do you wish your niece to have an education?"

"I do."

"Then bring her in to me and I shall judge how we can best help her."

"Something I ought to warn you about, Miss Parker. Jessica isn't quite right."

She cocked her head, a question in her eyes.

Slocum said, "First off, she's a half-breed. Her mother was a Snake Indian. Second, she got took advantage of."

"A man, Mr. Slocum? How old did you say she was?"

"She's fifteen years of age. There were three of them. They had her by force."

"I see." Miss Parker replaced her glasses. "I shall still need to see her," she said.

"I brought her. She's just outside."

Jessica and Miss Parker talked for an hour while Slocum cooled his heels in the outer office. Jessica had gone into the interview just like always, head down, leaden-footed, perhaps a little sullen. When she came out, the tips of her ears were beet-red. Miss Parker had more color in her face, too, like she'd been excited.

"I can pay good money for her tuition," Slocum said.

"She will cost you no more then the other girls," Miss Parker said. "She starts Monday."

Jessica was quiet all the way to the carriage. The coachman cracked his whip and the carriage rattled back toward the hotel.

"Well?" Slocum asked.

Jessica shook her head stubbornly.

"You gonna tell me what she said?"

"She said to buy my schoolbooks at Worden's Store," Jessica said. After a moment she added, "Miss Parker said I been acting like a coward."

John Slocum snapped his mouth shut and didn't say a word.

Jessica threw herself into her books with all the ardor of a first-time scholar. After more inquiries, John Slocum hit on a plan for Lacey, too. One afternoon, while Jessica was at school, he walked the boy down to the railroad's locomotive sheds and introduced him to a shop foreman dressed in shirt and tie. "If you take the apprenticeship," the foreman said, "you'll start as an oiler. It's a filthy, dangerous job. If you stick with it, you can become a fireman, or perhaps work here in the car barns. There's a future for you with the railroad."

Lacey looked at John Slocum for a decision.

"It's your life, son," Slocum said. "Seems to me you ain't had a lot of preparation for doing anything else. Unless," he added, "you really enjoy sweeping out saloons."

So the boy started as an oiler. The first couple of days he complained about the difficulty of the work, his fellow workers, and the impossible demands made on him. By the end of the week he was leaving for work early and whistling as he packed his lunch.

In the evening the three of them took dinner together. John Slocum was playing a little poker in the afternoons, just to keep his hand in. Over supper he talked of the men who sat to play with him. He spoke of the high rollers, the tinhorns, the bad men and good. He described their habits. He gave the two half-breeds the benefits of his own education. Lacey asked questions and, patiently, John Slocum gave answers. Jessica ate quickly and quietly then disappeared into her books. Late at night—very late—Slocum's detectives reported to him, telling him of Little Will, Jack, and Varese. Slocum listened, gave new instructions to his watchers, and waited.

John Slocum was unfailingly polite to Jessica Tripp, who was unfailing polite to him. Nothing more than that—just polite.

One rainy night in June—it was nearly eleven o'clock and both of the kids were in bed—John Slocum dressed in an impeccable suit, fawn in color, with a silk-lined cape and opera hat. He clipped a Remington double derringer to his wrist but left his Colt Navy in the dresser drawer. Softly he passed through the hotel lobby, past the dozing clerk. He awoke the first hack in line and told him, "River House."

It was a rainy miserable night, and the few cabs abroad splashed mud on each other. The clip-clip-clop of the horse's hooves, the hoot of steamboat whistles in the distance.

The lanterns outside the River House steamed and the

doorman swung the door open with a courteous remark about the awful weather.

"Yes." That was all Slocum said but he pressed a five-dollar gold piece into the doorman's hand and if he meant to protest the passage of a non-guest up the broad stairs of the River House, he looked at the coin in his hand and turned his back.

Lord Japhe awoke to the rasp of a lucifer. "Who?" He sat bolt upright in bed as the sputtering flare of his lantern settled into sustained burning. The bedside lamp threw the intruder's shadow against the far wall, looking gargantuan. "Sir! How dare you!"

The intruder stood back so the lamplight would play on his features. He was empty-handed, well-dressed, relaxed.

"John Slocum!"

"Yes. I've come for an answer to a question. Jessica couldn't or wouldn't say how many men raped her. Were you in on it?"

"Rape? Who? When?"

John Slocum's eyes seemed to glow in the lamplight. Lord Japhe felt like his soul was in the balance. At last the dark-haired man said, "I see. I thought so, but I had to be sure. My apologies, Lord Japhe."

As he turned to go, the Englishman called out, "Stay! I must know—*was* that girl Jessica raped?"

John Slocum turned, one hand on the doorknob. "Sir, I beg your pardon, but I don't think you want to know."

The Englishman slipped his pince-nez over his nose. His hair was tousled and his flannel nightshirt looked faintly ridiculous, but his voice had authority. "Slocum, I beg of you. If what I fear is true, then I must know it. If my son was not involved in this black deed, then I should be grateful and try to make up to him for my previous misjudgments. But if he was involved..."

"I'm sorry."

Lord Japhe lowered his head. Staring at the counterpane,

he said, "There has always been a wildness in the Japhe blood. In the old times, in Devonshire, the Japhes were more cursed than blessed. Little Will shall have nothing more from me."

Slocum said nothing.

"And the girl? Does she live, then?" the nobleman asked.

"She's right here in St. Louis. I've got her in school. I never had no special education, but I can see how it might do her some good."

The English lord's face grew brighter. He wanted to know everything about the girl. John Slocum took a seat and the two men continued their discussion for several hours. When Slocum slipped out of Lord Japhe's room, the two knew and respected each other as men.

The next day, over the evening meal, John Slocum explained his plan to the two kids. "I'll need your help," he said.

Jessica put down her implements neatly, the way she had been taught.

"I mean to have those gents," Slocum said, "for what they did to you and—"

"I can kill my own snakes," the boy snapped. "I already saved up enough for a pistol."

Slocum weighed the boy carefully before he said mildly, "They may have raped your sister, son, but they *killed* my horse. Who do you think has the prior claim?" With that difficulty disposed of, he enlisted them. The boy was to decoy Vinegar Varese.

It didn't prove difficult. Three times Lacey showed himself to Vinegar. Lord Japhe was asked to get Vinegar Varese to St. Stephen's on Sunday and found it no great difficulty. When Jessica and Lacey sang in the choir—arranged through Lord Japhe again—Vinegar went mad, rushing toward the choir stall like God himself was accusing.

The boy lured Vinegar Varese to the front door of the River House, where John Slocum shot him down. Vinegar fell to his knees with his life ebbing through his bloody clasped fingers while the carriage galloped away down the street.

It had happened so quickly that no man knew how or by whom the deed had been done. A few men knew the corpse was Little Will's friend, and they called Will away from his drinking to Vinegar's body stretched out in the wagon outside.

"Can't you see I'm having fun?" Little Will snarled. "What was he to me, anyway?"

The man who'd hauled Vinegar in hopes of some little reward described the details of the shooting: an unknown assailant with a hansome cab.

"Get out of here. Tip him in the river," Will said.

So Vinegar Varese made his last trip down the river. Parts of him got as far as South Vicksburg.

That evening, Lacey Tripp went to bed early. He said he wasn't feeling so good. He hadn't made much of a show with his dinner, just pushed it around his plate. John Slocum said nothing. The boy's first killing. There was nothing to say.

Jessica asked for seconds. The two of them sat in the soft summer evening. The hotel was well built and they could hear nothing in the halls. The window was slightly open for the smell of the flowers and the sound of the whippoorwill.

"It was like Lacey said." Jessica turned her eyes to his. "You were doing that man a favor."

Slocum smiled. "I reckon so. He didn't see it that way."

"I am glad he is dead." She dabbed at her lips and laid her napkin beside the plate, just like Miss Parker had taught her. "He is one less man who saw my shame."

Since this was the first time she'd talked about the rape, John Slocum set his elbows on the table and waited for more.

"The three of them used me in a way of love, but they

did not love me. It was hatred, what they did. They were trying to kill my heart and they nearly did. Though I could walk, afterwards, it was not the same. Before then, even in the winter, the world was full of color. They made me put those colors away. Before, the world was full of laughter. They made me see the sneer behind every laugh. They brought death to live in my belly and my womb. As you kill them, I shall live."

She stood then, in the cool of the evening, and unbuttoned her schoolgirl braces. Her eyes stayed on his. Calm eyes, full of resolve. "Come to my bed," she said. "Show me love where hatred has died."

She was so finely built he feared he would hurt her when he penetrated. Her eyes saw his eyes, devoured them. "Oh," she said, surprised.

He lay there then, drinking her in, quiet on her body, feeling her quiver around him, tremble under him, feeling the electricity in the palms of her hands. His neck hairs stood up when she touched them.

She stroked him like he was a cat and when he began diving deeper into her, she stroked him like she might stroke a horse, kneading his muscles in her strong little hands.

When she came, her belly rippled against his. A moment later she sucked in her gut and grunted and beat her heels against the back of his legs and cut him with her fingernails.

He held her for a long time after they had finished while the flush drained from her face and the palms of her hands. He held her until she slept, and when he slipped from her bed, she curled up against her pillow, innocent as a schoolgirl.

It would be just the one time. He knew that it would never happen again. She had used him.

He took a chair beside the window. Stars were out, scant moon. In the distance he could see the faint glow that marked St. Louis. It always surprised him how much light men used at night. Other critters just went to sleep, but man had to have all the lights burning. Of all the predators, men were the most afraid.

In a clear hand Slocum wrote out the terms of his will. After burial expenses, everything was to go to Lacey and Jessica. He signed the slip of paper and folded it into the saddlebag where he kept his gold. Tomorrow would be a fast day. He lifted the glass, blew out the lantern, and slept like a baby.

At six came a discreet knock on the hotel door. A clerk's voice called out that it was time. A coffeepot was waiting outside the door, just like he'd asked for.

Coffee at his elbow, he pulled the charges on his Colt and reloaded, carefully measuring his powder, centering his patches, settling the caps just so. He loaded all six. Going up against two men, he might need the edge.

He drank his coffee hot and black, selected a neat white shirt, and put a buff on his dark brown boots. His pants were dark blue twill, cavalry blue.

He tied down his holster with a neat double bow. The holster was hanging cross-draw, the way he favored. He thonged the Colt's hammer.

Yesterday he'd bought a second Colt, another Navy. It wasn't as fine tuned as the old one he'd had. The hammer was stiff and the trigger a touch heavier than he liked, but it'd do for a back-up. He pushed the second Colt in the back of his pants, set for a left-handed draw. His right hand would be awfully busy.

It was chilly enough for a jacket, and Slocum draped his over his shoulders like a cape. He set his hat just so.

Lord Japhe was waiting, just as he'd promised. The nobleman was dressed in his severest black and he looked to John Slocum like an executioner or a priest. There was something awfully fine-drawn in the older man's face, like he was connected to something other-worldly.

"G'morning."

"Yes." Lord Japhe pushed the carriage door open and

Slocum clambered in. "You decided not to bring the Tripps?"

"No. I believe they have had enough of this. Lacey's had his revenge, and Jessica don't need it."

Lord Japhe shot him a glance but didn't press the question. "And you?" he asked.

"I expect I ain't satisfied."

Lord Japhe sighed. "And yet you have suffered less than either Jessica or her brother."

"They killed my horse," Slocum said.

The two men looked at each other. It was Slocum who turned his face toward the morning. "I'll call it off if you ask me to," he said.

Lord Japhe's face was fierce. He'd inherited his share of that Japhe bad blood, at least as much as his son had. "I'll leave it in God's hands," Japhe said. "It's up to Him to punish or release."

"Him and Colonel Colt," Slocum said.

Lord Japhe offered Slocum a slug of good whiskey from his silver flask but Slocum felt fine, plenty warm, light as a feather. He wasn't thinking about anything particularly, just enjoying the way the light danced on the river and the bullrushes swaying.

"I'll be glad to leave St. Louis," Lord Japhe said.

"Going home?"

"Fastest train, fastest ship," the gentleman admitted.

"I'm headed west myself," Slocum said. "I never have seen the Sierra Nevadas."

They rode in silence then, each man lost in his own thoughts. A couple of wading birds in the shallows. Passenger pigeons chittering in the big elms. It was going to be a fine day and John Slocum's bones felt good. A sleepy bee flew in the window of the carriage and landed on his leg. The furry gold bee rested upon his dark trousers. After a brief exploration, the bee lifted off again.

The carriage followed the river road. Roadhouses, a ramshackle livery, the shot tower high above the new federal armory, scattered warehouses and tied up barges.

In the flood plain the cattails rose high as a man's head, a waving ocean of green. The road followed a bank and during high water only the road stayed above the river.

Half an hour south, their driver drew up before a gray building hanging partway over the water. A dozen horses were tied outside. A trickle of smoke came from the tin chimney. Big windows with real panes of glass facing the road were closed with a dark green curtain.

An ill-dressed man came through the door, fell to one knee, got up, fell to both knees, and got up and grabbed his horse and clung to the reins. His eyes saw the two men in the carriage but his brain did not.

Slocum said, "They'll be here. It's where they finish up their nights."

The drunk got on his horse and passed out along its neck without untying the reins.

"What a dismal spot." Lord Japhe shuddered.

John Slocum watched a couple of teals beat their way aloft on the river. "Depends how you look at it."

John Slocum got down and shut the door on Lord Japhe. The Englishman sat above the fighting ground like a judge.

Slocum's boots squished in the mud. He was plenty warm enough and left his cumbersome jacket at the coachman's feet. He turned his shoulders and flexed his fingers. He rolled a quirly while he looked the place over and popped a lucifer against the side of his boot. The smoke was sweet in his lungs.

The clapboard building was longer over the water than it was wide. By the evidence of rotting posts, it might have been a warehouse once.

The Colt slipped into John Slocum's hand and he shot the tin cap off the tin chimney.

The report drifted off down the river, finding a thin echo somewhere. Slocum let the pistol dangle in his hand. He felt the familiar chill across his neck that always came to him just before the fighting got underway.

The roadhouse door hurled open. Big, pot-bellied, angry-faced gent with a scattergun. "Hey! What you mean—"

John Slocum smiled and the man shut up. The pot-bellied gent pointed the scattergun away from the smiling, well-dressed, quiet man with the Colt in his fist. "Little Will! Mountain Jack! Come out and play!" The man and the scattergun scuttled back inside.

Mountain Jack came into the daylight, his hand shadowing his eyes.

"You look like hell, Jack," Slocum said.

That was true enough. Jack hadn't shaved in a week or two and his hair hung over his collar. He wore a flat-crowned hat hanging behind his neck and kept a greasy bandana stuffed into his shirt where a neckerchief or tie ought to be. He scratched his armpit and wrinkled up his face. "Do I know you?"

Little Will appeared just behind Jack. His pants were cleaner than Jack's and his boots had seen attention but he hadn't shaved either, and his little eyes were red-rimmed and mean. He looked right past Slocum to the carriage. "Father!" he gasped.

Lord Japhe didn't return the greeting or even acknowledge it. He just watched.

"I've come for you gentlemen," Slocum said.

Recognition began to dawn on Mountain Jack's befuddled face. His mouth dropped. "I know you," he said. "You're that damn rustler..."

"That's what you called me," Slocum said. "But that was a lie. You don't have many friends the other side of this river," Slocum said.

"Well, then." A smile played across Jack's features. He wasn't bored now.

"Do you have business with us?" Little Will asked. Little Will turned away slightly and his right hand stole behind his back, seeking the revolver he always kept there. Mountain Jack flexed his fingers and his grin deepened. He began a casual drift off to the right, in front of those big windows, his hand at his side.

"My business is your death," John Slocum said, quite reasonably.

Little Will giggled, a high, rather childish giggle. He must have astounded himself, because he pressed the back of his left hand across his mouth. His right was still sneaking his gun.

"I disown you," his father said. "You are not my son."

"Oh, hell," Little Will said. "Who cares?"

"You shouldn't have come after me," Slocum said. "You shouldn't have hurt that girl."

"There's two of us," Little Will said. "You won't be able to deal with both of us." Little Will took a step to his left. The space between him and Mountain Jack must have been twenty feet. "By the time you kill one of us, the other one will have you." Little Will's pistol touched his hand like it was surprised to be there. Little Will's thumb found the hammer. "Jack's been practicing every day. He's the fastest man along the river. He'll kill you before you can do any harm." That calm sideways movement, like a supple sidewinder snake.

Slocum slipped into the gunfighter's crouch, leaned slightly forward to take a bullet, hunched low to deliver one. "Make your play," he whispered.

Somehow, it had never occurred to Little Will that he could hurt so bad. The worst pain he'd known as a child was when his pony fell and he suffered a broken ankle. The bullets that hammered the life out of him were terrible, terrible pain, and he quite forget about the pistol in his hand. He died to escape the pain.

Mountain Jack was very fast. He got off one shot, though it flew harmlessly away and never hit anything. Mountain Jack left this life feeling bad. He died with his boots on.

JAKE LOGAN